THE FALLING KIND

By Randileigh Kennedy

Thanks for reading my book!

Hope you enjoy it! :)

~ Randileigh Kennedy

To M.F. - the only boy I've ever truly fallen for.

CHAPTER 1

"Sydney, can you watch the front desk real quick while I head back to the break room? I have to get rid of the bodies before anyone finds out," Eva said with a scrunched up face.

"I hope that's some terrible joke," I countered. Usually phrases like that weren't thrown loosely around the vet clinic.

"I did it again," she said frantically. "The entire Consuelo family is floating."

I popped my head around the hallway door where I had a direct line of sight to the staff room. Sure enough, the rectangular fish tank she kept on the counter was eerily calm. The water looked far cloudier than usual – likely the cause of the massacre.

"I already killed the Rodriguez family last month," she said, pointing towards the tank. "The Mendez family didn't make it long before that. Dr. Nikki is going to think I'm an idiot."

Sadly my first thought was that she might need to start watching a new telenovela for more name inspiration if she planned on getting another batch. For some reason she named them all after her favorite soap opera characters.

"How is it that you are employee of the month time after time, but yet you can't keep your own fish alive?" I teased. It was quite ironic, given our line of work. Eva was just the receptionist at the clinic, she wasn't a vet tech like me, but I still found it amusing.

"Will you please just watch the front for me? It will take less than ten minutes," she said, making her way towards the back. She rummaged through a room down the hall and pulled out a plastic bag and a small net. The nice thing about working the late shift at the clinic was how slow it was at night. Sometimes an hour or more would pass without a single walk-in. It wasn't my usual shift, or Eva's for that matter, but we were covering tonight for some other co-workers.

"No one is coming in this late, it's almost closing time," I said, checking the white clock in the lobby area. I threw my long blonde hair up into a loose ponytail. "It's already nine forty-five. I'll help you," I said sincerely, reaching out for one of the items she held.

She handed me the plastic bag, which meant she planned to scoop out the bodies. We made our way to the break room and she removed the lid from the tank. With a disgusted face, she scooped the net in and plopped the wet, heaping pile into my outstretched plastic bag. Water splashed all over my hands, and I couldn't help but scrunch up my face at the aroma. It was a mixture of chemicals and sea death.

"How can they possibly smell so bad this quickly?" I asked as she dropped in a second scoop. At that same moment, the front door chime sounded.

I walked up to the lobby area, forgetting I had the plastic bag of decay still in my hands. As I made it to the front desk, I noticed two men and a whole lot of blood.

"Eva," I yelled back towards the break room, "I'm going to need some assistance." It appeared the dead fish were the least of our problems tonight.

I quickly assessed the two men as they approached me. They had blood all over their arms, but they didn't appear to be holding an injured animal. The taller man was young with a large, strong frame and a worried expression. He had short messy light brown hair and tan skin. The older man with him had a long silver braid and a weathered face. He was clearly of Indian descent. I could tell by the look in his eyes that he was in pain. I noticed he was holding a blood-soaked area near his ribs.

"Was there an accident?" Eva said frantically, dropping her wet fish net on the wooden desk. "Where's your animal?"

"No animals," the young man said calmly. I noticed a huge gash on his left forearm. "There was just a little incident outside your office. Harvey needs medical attention."

Eva immediately dialed 911 from her desk phone.

"What happened? Are there others, or just the two of you?" I asked. I'd been working in the vet clinic for nearly four years and I'd seen a lot of horrible wounds. This much blood up close on humans, however, threw me for a loop. I felt helpless.

"I can get you some towels?" I offered. "Maybe some antiseptic? Did you get cut with something?" My words felt somewhat distorted in my head like I wasn't asking the right questions.

"Just a little bit of metal," Harvey replied with a forced smile, still clutching his ribs.

"Was the piece of metal a knife?" Eva chimed in, looking at each of the men. "That looks serious, you're dripping blood all over the floor."

I quickly made my way to the back of the office, washing my hands and grabbing some towels and disposable pads.

"The ambulance is two minutes out," Eva stated, helping me with the towels in my arms. She gently held one up to Harvey's torso, trying to maneuver it towards his wound without causing more pain.

"Here," I said to the younger man, wrapping a towel around his forearm. "Apply some pressure."

"Thanks," he replied sincerely. "Really, mine looks worse than it is. I'm more worried about Harvey. He needs to get to the hospital. My bike is out front, but I didn't think he'd be able to hold on to steady himself."

I couldn't imagine these two men riding all the way to Mountain Ridge Memorial Hospital on a bicycle. It was only a few minutes away by car, but it would've been a disastrous attempt with Harvey's torso bleeding like it was.

It felt like it was mere seconds before the ambulance sirens were right out front of our clinic. Two EMTs rushed through the front door.

"Are you sure you're fine? Can you head back to the warehouse tonight?" Harvey asked the younger guy with a strained expression.

"Yeah, I'll take care of the delivery tonight," he said calmly with a nod. "I'll come by the hospital after it's done."

"Sir, you're injured too?" one of the EMTs probed while the other ushered Harvey to the ambulance.

"Oh, uh, no, I just got a little scratch. I'm fine," he replied, relaxing his broad shoulders. "This nice lady here," he continued, gesturing towards me, "I'm sorry, I didn't get your name…"

"Sydney Summers," I interjected awkwardly.

"Yes, Sydney took care of me, I'm fine. Just Harvey needs the help, but thank you," he said politely. The blood from his arm was already seeping through the towel I gave him moments ago.

"I would still advise you to come with us to get it looked at, but if not," the EMT explained, pushing a piece of paper towards the desk counter, "I'm going to need you to sign this refusal. What's your name?"

"Cole Mason," the guy responded, moving his left arm away to hide the wound. "I'll sign, thank you." He grabbed the EMT's pen with his right hand and scribbled his signature on the piece of paper in front of him. Harvey was already out in the ambulance, ready to go. The EMT nodded at the three of us and left the clinic. Seconds later, the sirens sounded again as they made their way towards the hospital. It all happened so quickly.

"Do you want me to call someone?" I offered towards him, unsure of what his plan was. "You really should get that looked at. It looks pretty bad. If you were a dog, I would sedate you," I said awkwardly.

He smiled back at me. "Like the way you sedated those fish?" he asked with a smirk, pointing to the plastic bag I dropped on the ground during all the commotion.

"That was an unfortunate freak accident," I said formally, feeling slightly embarrassed. "I'm probably supposed to point out that this is in no way a representation of our clinic. Who do you want me to call?" I asked again, trying to redirect the conversation. I felt my cheeks blush for some reason.

"The only person I would call is Harvey, but he's worse off than I am," he replied lightly. "Honestly I'm fine."

I hadn't noticed that Eva left at any point, but she emerged from the back room with a mop and some new towels.

"I'll take care of this," Eva offered, pointing to the drips of blood on the lobby floor. "You guys can get out of here. You have the early shift tomorrow, don't you?" she asked.

"Yeah, I'm here at six a.m. I was just covering tonight for Lisa," I answered. "But I'll help you."

"No, I should be doing this, it's my mess," Cole interjected, reaching out to take the mop. "I'm really sorry for all the trouble tonight."

"It'll take five minutes," Eva scoffed, shooing Cole's outstretched arm away. "But I can't walk you home Syd, so maybe he can do that for me? Just to make sure you get home all right?"

Ah, now I get it. Eva was trying to play matchmaker despite these weird, bloody circumstances. It was like she was forever waiting for one of her telenovelas to play out in real life. Unfortunately, I doubted any of them started this way.

"It's three blocks, I'll be fine," I said with a slight laugh. I had to admit, now that my attention was taken off of the emergent situation of two bloody strangers, Cole did have a nice face. His eyes were a light blue-green and he had a dimple in his left cheek when he smiled. I could do far worse. Although I was definitely off dating for the time being.

"Come on, get out of here," Eva repeated, waving her hands toward the front door. "I'll lock up."

I grabbed another small towel from the pile on the front desk and gently placed it around Cole's left forearm to catch any additional blood before he made it home, just as a precaution.

"Which way are you headed?" he asked courteously as I grabbed my purse from behind the counter.

"Up Savannah," I replied, studying his face. I really didn't need an escort; Mountain Ridge was an extremely safe town nestled around Lake Tahoe. There really wasn't a lot of crime. Although whatever had happened to Harvey and Cole, that didn't sit well with me. Something bad must've taken place right out front of the clinic.

"I'm headed that way anyway. I'd love to walk with you," he said politely. He smiled and that stupid cheek dimple pulled me in. I could probably stand to walk five minutes with this guy. And honestly if there was any trouble around here, his size alone would be a deterrent. Although that apparently didn't work out so well for him just minutes ago.

I said goodbye to Eva, and while Cole's back was turned she mouthed '*O.M.G.*' and made a dramatic eye gesture towards me. I grinned, mildly amused by her reaction to him. I debated whether I would make up a good soap opera-worthy story about our walk home, or whether I would just tell her the truth, which would likely be that our brisk stroll ended with a simple goodbye and no further exchange.

As we walked outside the vet clinic, I noticed a silver-grey motorcycle parked next to the building. It seemed oddly placed for this time of night. Not a lot happened around this area at ten p.m.

"I'll move it before you open in the morning, I promise," he stated, picking up on my curiosity.

"That's yours?" I replied with a surprised tone.

"Yeah. Would you prefer a ride home?" he asked with a raised brow.

"Oh my gosh, I feel like an idiot," I laughed. "When you said you had a bike, I thought you meant an actual bike. Like with spokes. Like you were planning to take Harvey to the hospital on your handlebars."

"I look like a bicycle rider to you?" he replied with an amused grin.

He wore a fitted grey v-neck t-shirt that hugged the shape of his very toned chest. His dark jeans hung loose from his hips. He looked very athletic, that was for sure. He had to be at least six-foot-four. He was quite a presence.

"You're right, I guess I wouldn't really picture you in neon spandex," I teased. Although as I said it, I had to admit my mind wandered a bit, imagining him in such an outfit. I quickly changed the subject. "Your arm's a mess. It's bleeding through the towel. Let's just walk, you shouldn't be on the bike tonight anyway until we can get it wrapped up properly."

He smiled at me and put his hands in his pockets, using his side to keep the towel in place as we headed east towards the street I lived on.

"Are you from around here originally?" he asked as we walked. The early July air was warm during the day, but this late at night it always had a crispness to it that I really enjoyed. It was far different than summers in the Midwest where I was from.

"I moved here for school," I answered. "I'm from Chicago. The vet at the clinic is a family friend, so she's the one who convinced me to head out this way. Lake Michigan is pretty, but honestly, I don't think I've ever seen a lake prettier than Tahoe. I love it here."

"Chicago, huh? You're a long way from home then," he replied, listening attentively. "Are your parents still there?"

"It's just my dad. My mom passed from cancer back when I was in high school. He finally retired last year and moved to Florida so he could golf year round. So this is my home now. There's nowhere to go back to," I said with a shrug. I felt like I was rambling.

I noticed he grabbed his left forearm as we walked. His eyes winced.

"I really do think you need medical attention," I mentioned, noting the blood still appeared to be soaking into the towel. "It looked like a pretty deep cut. Do you want a ride to the hospital? We can grab my car and…"

"No, really," he said, cutting me off. "It's better if I don't. I don't exactly have health insurance right now. Plus they'll ask me all sorts of questions. I really think it's better if I just take care of it on my own."

"Well at the very least it needs to be cleaned out," I explained. "But you may need stitches. Do you want me to take a look at it?" I wasn't sure exactly what I was offering him. I dealt with animals, not people. I probably couldn't even help him. But I felt bad for him and it seemed right to offer some sympathy and take a quick look at it.

"I don't want to impose on your night," he said politely. "You've already helped quite a bit."

"This is me," I said pointing to a modest two-story condo. It had a brick exterior and pretty outdoor lighting, but the inside was a bit dated. The rent was decent though, which was helpful since I now had student loans to pay off. The real selling points for me however were the upstairs patio and the fact that the landlord let me have pets – which was a must for my current work situation. "Do you want to come in? I can take a look at your arm real quick."

"Only for a minute," he replied. "I really don't want to keep you up late."

Honestly I wasn't sure why I was inviting this guy in. He was a complete stranger. Not to mention he was just stabbed ten minutes ago. His lack of distress about it led me to believe the stabbing wasn't a total fluke or a totally unwarranted violent crime. Since when did a tight v-neck t-shirt and a new wound portray honesty and trustworthiness? Yet I didn't feel an ounce of trepidation in my entire body.

I slid the key in the lock and opened the front door, motioning him to follow me in. He smiled and obliged.

"Do you live alone? Or…" he began, then hesitated.

Yep. The exact question asked before you're about to be murdered.

"Not exactly," I snickered as a loud squeal came from the living room.

"You have a baby?" he questioned, sounding completely caught off guard.

I couldn't help but laugh. "No, just a mini pig. And two cats. And two rabbits."

"Whoa, that's quite the family," he teased.

"None of them are mine, it's just temporary," I explained. "When the local animal shelter gets to capacity they call us. Usually we have some kennels at the clinic to help them out, but sometimes there's a bit of an overflow."

"So you take them all home with you?" he said smiling.

"Just until they can be placed in proper homes," I continued. "They have nowhere else to go. I can't just abandon them, we have to do something. At least in the meantime I'm able to work with them, train them, socialize them…"

"How do you socialize a pig?" he asked with an amused smirk.

"Those are actually easy," I continued, setting my purse down on the small side table next to my couch. I turned on a few lights. I opened up the make-shift baby gate pen I had set up between the kitchen and the living room and the small fifteen pound pig ran out. "This is Dexter." As soon as Cole reached out an arm to touch him, the pig flopped over on his side, expecting a belly rub. Cole laughed and began scratching the pig's stomach.

"This is the weirdest thing I've ever experienced," he said, looking entertained.

"You were stabbed tonight, and *this* is unusual?" I snickered. I walked into the kitchen and pulled out a pre-made salad I had in the fridge. I set it down and Dexter came running.

"Come on, let me see that arm," I said softly, walking him into the kitchen. He laid his arm down on the center island and I washed my hands quickly in the sink. After patting them dry, I reached out and slowly began unwrapping the soaked towel layers. He sucked in his breath and I could tell it hurt.

"How bad is it?" he questioned.

"It's deeper than I thought," I replied truthfully. "You're going to need stitches."

"Can you do that?" he asked seriously. "Don't you do that kind of thing at the vet?"

I laughed nervously. "Well I'm just a vet tech, so I don't do the actual stitching."

"Well you've probably watched it hundreds of times, right?"

I looked up at him, trying to gauge just how serious he was. "Yes. I've watched the vet do them. But I'm not authorized to perform those types of services. I've never done it."

"I trust you," he said, still maintaining eye contact with me.

"Are you kidding? I just said I've never done it before and you want me to stitch up your arm? I think you're in shock," I said sarcastically. "You shouldn't let strangers put needles in you. Didn't your parents teach you anything?"

"Well my father was stabbed tonight. So if I'm being honest, maybe he's not the best judge of character."

"Harvey is your dad?" I asked, feeling completely confused. There was no resemblance whatsoever, and Harvey looked quite a bit older – maybe more like a grandfather. Cole didn't look like an Indian with his light eyes and light brown hair. There had to be more to that story.

"It's complicated," he said hesitantly. He didn't elaborate, suggesting to me that he didn't want to talk about it any further. "Look, you just fed a house pig a salad. I don't believe there's anything you can't do." He smiled at me and I couldn't help but stare back at his face.

"I have some antiseptic… some hydrogen peroxide, gauze…" I rambled, trying to think what supplies I really had in an old First-Aid kit I kept in the bathroom upstairs. "I can at least clean it out for you," I said with a shrug.

He was still smiling at me with such a soft, genuine expression. "I trust you," he repeated. "Whatever you feel comfortable with."

I headed upstairs and pulled out my First-Aid kit. I rummaged through it, noting the contents. It was fuller than I thought, but I wasn't sure how much of it was really useful for this situation. Some of the creams inside were probably expired already. I closed the box back up and carried it downstairs.

"So it looks like I have a few things, but…" I stopped talking when I realized Cole was no longer in my kitchen. I looked around the condo. The guest bathroom door was open and the light was off, so he wasn't in there. The back sliding door was still locked like it was earlier.

The empty end table next to my couch caught my attention – my purse was gone.

Son of a bitch. I was robbed.

Apparently guys with tight v-neck t-shirts and stab wounds weren't to be trusted after all.

CHAPTER 2

Exhausted and frustrated, I reemerged back downstairs in my tiny satin sleep shorts and a thin camisole. My condo felt unusually warm, unless that was just my feelings of anger and stupidity rising to the surface. Who lets a random crime victim into their house? I was such an idiot. This was exactly why I preferred animals to humans.

I retied my long blonde hair back into a tighter ponytail and stretched out onto the couch, turning on the TV. I needed to unwind before bed. My nerves were on fire.

Seconds later, my front door opened.

Maybe, just maybe, I peed a little.

I immediately jumped off the couch and into some pseudo karate-style pose.

Cole just stood there, looking dumbfounded.

"I'm sorry, did I scare you?" he asked, looking completely confused.

"What the hell are you doing?" I shrieked, trying to catch my breath.

"I just stepped outside for a phone call. It was the hospital, calling about Harvey," he explained, still looking a bit bewildered by what he just walked in on. "Were you going to karate chop me?" His mouth curled up into an innocent smirk.

"I thought you robbed me and left," I stated, still breathing hard. "I thought you were gone and I was alone, so then I, and I, and then you came…" I couldn't get my words out. I wasn't totally sure what I thought was just about to happen to me.

"Why would I rob you?" he said with a boyish smile. "You're supposed to be saving my life with your First-Aid kit. What would I take from you, the pig? He's still here." Dexter was snoring under a pile of blankets in the corner. At least I had learned just now that pigs weren't good security animals.

"My purse was on the table," I said, pointing to the side of the couch.

"Yeah, and while you were upstairs, Dexter jumped up on the couch and was trying to eat it. He was after a bag of muffins you had in there. So I grabbed the purse from him and hung it up on your coat hook." He pointed to a small wooden plank of hooks I had hanging up by the hall closet. Sure enough, my purse was hanging up next to one of my sweatshirts.

"I'm such an idiot," I muttered, shaking my head. "Sorry." I rested a hand on my hip, just to realize I was barely dressed.

Cole apparently noticed it too. "I like that outfit better than the scrubs," he mused, "if I'm being honest. Although the scrubs made me feel safer, particularly if you're performing surgery on me."

"Oh my gosh, I'm practically naked," I said in a panic, plucking up a pillow from the couch. Unfortunately that didn't really help. "One minute. Don't leave and freak me out all over again."

"This is Nevada you know, you actually have more clothes on than most women around here," he said lightheartedly.

In about forty-five seconds I came back downstairs in a soft, thin knee-length robe. Although I knew it would get hot with the extra layer, I figured he wouldn't be staying long enough for it to matter anyway.

"Back to the kitchen," I directed, opening up the First-Aid kit on the counter. "First rinse it off in the sink to get most of the blood off and then I'll disinfect it."

Cole walked over to the sink and turned on the water. I watched his muscles as they flexed while rubbing his forearm. His physique itself looked intimidating. I could see tattoos on his biceps sticking out of the bottom of his sleeves. I wondered if he had others elsewhere. The softness of his smile though made him seem more approachable. Not necessarily my type, but not exactly someone I'd run away from either.

Once most of the blood was rinsed off his arm I joined him next to the sink. I took a fresh hand towel and gently padded his wound.

"Can't we use the towels from the clinic? I don't want to get blood on yours," he said thoughtfully.

"Those ones are pretty saturated. It's fine, they're just towels," I said reassuringly. I continued to gently press on his deep cut, trying to assess just how bad it was. "I still think you need stitches, but there is a zero percent chance of me trying that on you. I do have some butterfly strips that might work though. If I completely disinfect it and we can close it up tonight, that may work. But you have to keep it clean at all times and use this on it several times a day," I explained, handing him some ointment. "You should still have someone look at it in the next two or three days though, just to make sure it's healing properly and to make sure you're not showing signs of infection."

"So, can I take you out to dinner on Tuesday?" he asked with a shy smile.

"You don't have to take me out to dinner," I replied back with a smirk. "You can stop by the clinic and I can have a look at it, if you're still refusing to have an actual doctor check it."

"But what if I wanted to take you to dinner? Would you go?" he asked with some apprehension in his voice. He stared straight into my blue eyes, waiting for an answer. My hands were still on his forearm but the feeling in my fingertips changed. I was suddenly more aware of my physical contact with his skin and it made me nervous.

"Well, I, yeah, I like dinner," I uttered. *What was I saying? 'I like dinner?'* I repeatedly sounded like a mumbling moron in front of this guy. "I mean it's not that I *wouldn't* go. But you don't have to take me out, we can just fix you up at the clinic. You don't have to take me out for this."

"But what if I wanted to? Like on an actual date," he specified.

"I'm not really in the market for dating," I continued to ramble. "I mean for starters, this is a horrible 'how we met' story. How do I tell my friends? First you were stabbed in front of my clinic, then I thought you robbed me, which turned into me thinking you came back to murder me, and then we went out for pizza? This just doesn't feel like a place where people end up on a date." *Stop talking,* I urged myself. "Honestly I'm off the market right now. I'm taking a break."

"Well you already met my family, Harvey, and I already saw you in your pajamas. We're practically on third base as it is," he said jokingly, lightening the mood. "Just tacos. We can keep it simple. We don't have to call it a date. I just want to properly thank you for what you've done for me."

"This is already third base?" I said nervously, hung up on those words. "I feel we're moving from tacos to completely misjudging the distance between third base and home plate. It's farther than you think, you know…" *What the hell was I saying now? I'm talking in baseball references? What, like I'm into sports all of a sudden? Not to mention the distance between all the bases is mathematically the same, right?* I wanted to shove all the gauze in my own mouth to get me to stop talking.

"Sorry, let's pretend like the last five minutes of my life never happened," I stated matter-of-factly, finally trying to gather my thoughts. "This is going to hurt by the way," I said, completely changing the subject. I poured the antiseptic over the open wound, and despite Cole trying not to flinch, I could see his jaw tighten and his fists flex. He still managed to smile at me through his clenched teeth and I appreciated his ability to hold it all in. I probably would've been screaming by this point - assuming the initial stab hadn't already done me in.

"Are you even going to tell me what happened to you tonight?" I questioned, trying to keep the subject off dinner.

"Right place, wrong time," he answered with a shrug. "Something like that." He again didn't elaborate, so I let it go.

"Well the bleeding seems controlled," I said as I continued to dry the area. Once all the moisture was out of his skin, I carefully applied eight butterfly strips to pull the skin closed. I wrapped it with some white gauze from the First-

Aid kit to keep it all together and tight for the time being. Once it was wrapped, I held up his forearm to inspect my work. It seemed well constructed from what I could tell, considering he was the first human I ever worked on.

"Thank you," he said softly. We both stood up from the kitchen barstools we were sitting on and I stepped back towards the kitchen cabinets. I threw all of the soiled towels into the trash, smirking when I saw the mangled package of muffins Dexter tried to eat from my purse. They were completely smashed. I washed my hands in the sink and dried them as Cole slowly made his way towards the front door.

"Sorry to keep you up so late. I know you have an early morning," he said with such a genuine, considerate tone.

"I'm sorry you had to see my threatening karate pose in my short shorts," I stated with a quiet laugh. I opened the front door for him and he gently brushed past me, turning to face me before stepping out.

"At least I know you're safe here," he replied sarcastically with a smile.

"Are you stopping by the hospital to check on Harvey or are you heading home?" I asked, not because I necessarily cared about the answer. For some reason I just wanted him to stay next to me a little longer.

"I've got a few things to do at Harvey's warehouse first. Then I'll head to the hospital after that," he replied, staring at me with intense eyes like he wasn't in a hurry to leave either. We stared at each other for what seemed like a full minute. His eyes looked full of so many secrets I wanted to know.

Without warning, he leaned up against me and pressed his lips to mine, lingering, waiting for my reaction. I couldn't help but kiss him back. His lips felt warm and full of purpose and I longed to feel more of them. I reached up and touched his firm bicep through his shirt and he put his hand on mine, squeezing it lightly. His lips continued to press against mine and he no longer felt like a stranger.

He slowly pulled back, relaxing his hand from mine. He gently brushed a stray section of hair back behind my ear.

"Goodnight Sydney," he whispered softly. "Lock your door after I leave."

"I will," I replied with a stupidly dreamy smirk on my face.

"Are you going to bed?" he asked as he slowly walked down my front steps.

"I don't know," I replied bashfully. "I think I may need to brush up on my baseball."

CHAPTER 3

The next morning my alarm chime at five a.m. did not thrill me. I sluggishly took a shower and tied my hair up in a loose wet bun. Fortunately my work attire options of lavender scrubs or teal scrubs made getting dressed an easy task. I always chose lavender when they were clean.

I ate some cereal and headed out around five forty-five. When I opened the front door, I smiled as I noticed a small stack of white hand towels sitting on top of my front steps with a small red bow. There was also a package of muffins propped up on top. I was amazed a raccoon hadn't run off with the food, although maybe they hadn't been sitting here long. Who knows what time he dropped them off. I bent down to pick them up, noticing a small piece of paper underneath the muffins.

I read the note.

If you ever find yourself thinking about ~~me~~ tacos, give me a call.

There was a phone number following. I snickered at his cross-out of the word 'me' – I definitely appreciated his sense of humor. There was more at the bottom of the note.

PS – Dexter probably isn't very remorseful about ruining your muffins, but I figured I should also replace those. ~ C

I smiled at the entire gesture. It was rather sweet, especially from a guy like Cole. Not that I knew him at all, but he just didn't look like a romantic guy. Granted, these were just towels and muffins, but still. It was relatively charming.

I began my short walk to the vet clinic. I wanted to stop thinking about Cole, I swear. I was serious about my lack of interest in dating. Even if I was to consider going out with someone, he didn't fit my usual interests. He looked, I don't know, too rugged for me. The motorcycle, the tattoos… The fact that he didn't even hesitate to trust me to stitch him up – it all just seemed a little suspect to me. Even his massive size was a far cry from guys I had dated in the past. He was huge. It all felt a little intimidating to me. Besides, I doubted we even had much in common.

I reached the clinic and turned my key in the door. I couldn't help but notice they grey motorcycle was gone from the lot. He must've had a long night.

"Tell me everything," my best friend Sam said, pulling her red Honda into the lot and immediately jumping out. We'd met in the dorms our sophomore year and we instantly clicked when we found out we had the same vet science major. She was from Oregon and had a bright, bubbly personality. Her dark auburn hair framed her heart shaped face with a trendy bob.

"Tell you about what?" I asked curiously as she followed me into the clinic in her teal scrubs. Sam wanted to branch out more into emergency surgery. She was currently taking summer classes to get ahead before moving back to Oregon for her Doctor of Veterinary Medicine. I had similar plans, but those all fell apart about a year ago. I hated thinking about it, both her moving and the fact that I wasn't sure what direction I was now headed.

"Oh come on, you know exactly what I'm talking about," she said with a smirk as we hung up our purses in the back room. "Didn't you go home last night with a gorgeous stranger? How did Eva put it… Something about the face of a movie star and the body of a Greek God? Why is it that I'm hearing about your love life from Eva?" she said with an animated expression.

"First off, I have no love life," I corrected her. "I'm keeping that at a level zero. Which point two, that's why I didn't even bother to call you last night. It was already late, and it's a non-story."

Sam pulled a small lunch bag out of her purse, setting it in our break room fridge. "Really Syd? You take a hot, muscular guy back to your condo and you have nothing for me? You're hopeless. And a disappointment," she snickered.

"It wasn't what you're imaging in your brain right now," I explained. "The guy was stabbed out front of the clinic. I just cleaned up his arm, that was it."

"So then he left, end of story? No phone number exchange? No making googly eyes at each other? No 'maybe I'll see you again the next time you get stabbed' future plans?" Sam asked skeptically. "Come on, give me *something*," she urged.

"It was too weird of a situation," I admitted. "When you meet someone for the first time, it's supposed to be some sweet 'it was nice running into you' kind of situation. Some mild flirting, discussing common interests, that kind of thing… This was not like that at all."

"So he literally just left? That was it?" she continued to pry.

"Well, he did kind of kiss me," I replied with a shrug. "Then I rambled on about baseball or something stupid, you know how I get when I'm nervous. He did try asking me to dinner, but I shut him down on that. I'm telling you, it just wasn't a normal situation."

"He kissed you? And that's a non-story?" she squealed loudly. "I agree, it sounds like a random sequence of events, but I'm so proud of you! That's pretty good progress, given you haven't kissed a guy since Ian."

"Please don't bring that up," I interjected, cutting her off. That wasn't a subject I liked talking about – ever. Especially not on a work day when I needed to maintain my composure. "Look, it was just a weird, random night. Nothing will come of it. Unless he comes to the clinic for me to check his arm, I doubt I'll even see him again. But it doesn't matter, he's not even my type at all."

"Of course not, why would handsome and muscular be your type?" she teased.

"Good morning ladies," Dr. Nikki said cheerfully, popping her head into the break room. "Sydney, you're going to kill me, but the message service was quite busy last night. The Humane Society has six new ones to bring over today, and we only have room here for four. Any chance you can handle a rabbit at your place, and one tortoise? It would just be for a couple of nights. I may have a home for Dexter by Friday, but unfortunately they're coming in faster than we have them going out."

Sadly, this was eternally our problem. The clinic already got fined once for being over capacity, so I knew she couldn't risk it again.

"Of course, I have an open spot for the rabbit for sure, I only have those two black spotted ones right now. As for the tortoise, that should be pretty low maintenance, right? I can probably keep him in the kitchen, high enough so Dexter can't get to him?" I offered. Dr. Nikki was so compassionate about all of these animals that I couldn't help but try and accommodate them for her. She kindly showed her appreciation by bringing me groceries when she dropped off food and toys for the animals, and occasionally my rent was even covered when I had a full house. She was so generous when I needed time off too, so I genuinely didn't mind helping her out in any way I could. Plus, it gave me some company.

"You are a lifesaver," she replied sincerely as she left the room.

"See, if you lived in an apartment with pet restrictions like me, you could have a normal dating life without pigs and tortoises running around," Sam teased. "Maybe that would help you find time for a guy."

"Your place is a dive, that's why you're always hanging out at mine," I joked back. "You *do* have pets already, they're called mice."

"Oh stop, it's not that bad. Besides, mice are cute," she happily shrugged. "Hey, are we still on for that concert tomorrow night?"

"Of course, looking forward to it. Beach today after work?" Many of our afternoons were spent the same way, lazily laying out in the summer sun, reading magazines and talking about life.

"Yep, I need to work on my tan before tomorrow night," she agreed. "Come on, we have a spay to prep for. Let's get to work."

The workday passed by pretty routinely. No major catastrophes, which was always a relief in our line of work. We unexpectedly adopted out a few rabbits and two cats to someone who owned a small farm, which would free up the ones I had in my condo. That would leave me with Dexter and the unnamed tortoise for the time being, probably the least amount of pets I ever had at one time.

Since Sam and I had the early shift, we got off at three in the afternoon. We loved days like that because the clinic was only a five minute walk down to the beach. Lake Tahoe had so many wonderful beaches, both on the Nevada side where we were and on the California side about twenty minutes away. But Halo Beach, the one nearest to the clinic and my apartment, was by far my favorite. There were no good parking spots near it, so it was mostly only locals versus the crowds of tourists most of the other Tahoe beaches had.

Sam and I brought the tortoise back to my place, securing his tank on top of my kitchen table far away from Dexter's curious snout. Sam made Dexter a giant salad for his late lunch and then we made our way down to the beach.

"We've gotta talk about this concert tomorrow night, what's the deal with this band guy?" I asked as we neared the water's edge. We laid out our towels and dropped our bags.

"Ah, Soul Punch," Sam replied dreamily.

"That's the band's name? Soul Punch? Is that a horrible joke?" I said with a giggle.

"Yeah, so not a great name," Sam agreed with a laugh. We laid down on our towels to take in the sunshine. "Honestly the band isn't even that great. But their guitarist…" she gushed.

Last week Sam had a date with a guy she met at the library. He took her to some dive bar and although she wasn't into the date, she left swooning over the guitar player. She never even got his name, but it was all she talked about over the last few days.

"So I've done a bit of internet stalking," Sam continued, "and I've narrowed down his name. It's either Tyler, Luke, Ethan, or Barry. Their crappy website didn't have them labeled, it only listed their names," she sighed.

"So where's the bar, what's the name again? Joe something?" I asked. I knew it wasn't a place I'd ever been to before.

"Local Joe's," she stated. "You're going to freak out when you see it, it's a total dive. But it appears to be the only place they play. Here's the bad part… It's in the West Cove."

"The snake pit?" I uttered. "We're going to get mugged."

"I know, not the best spot. But at least it's on a Tuesday night. That has to be better than a weekend, right?" she speculated.

"I don't know, the fact that this band can only book a weeknight in some crappy bar, that's just bad all around. How terrible are these guys?"

"It's bad," she admitted. "But I'm telling you, when you see the guitarist, it will all make sense. It will be worth risking our lives for in some seedy dive bar." She giggled.

There was an area nearby known as the West Cove. It was still on the Nevada side of Lake Tahoe, but it was nestled into the trees right near the California line. Nothing good happened in West Cove, according to the nightly news anyway. It was riddled with dive bars, cheap motels, and run down trailers and cabins. It was such an odd little pocket of Mountain Ridge life. The rest of the lake towns were full of tourists or multi-million dollar homeowners who dwelled in huge five-story mansions on the lake. There was still a strong working middle class area across from the lakefront owners – people like me in modest condos or duplexes. But crime in general was really low in this beautiful town full of outdoor enthusiasts. West Cove was the black hole of the entire area.

"The bar itself isn't as bad inside as it looks on the outside," Sam commented, shrugging it off. "I wouldn't exactly go there alone, but in reality it's only a few miles from here. Maybe Brandt can come with us."

"Yeah, because he looks tough and threatening," I said sarcastically. Brandt was my ex's best friend. Even though Ian was very much out of the picture, Brandt and I remained pretty close. Along with Sam, the three of us did a lot together.

"You're right, we need a real bodyguard. Maybe the guy from the clinic?" Sam suggested. "Eva said he's literally a giant mass of muscle. That would serve us well," she said with a smile.

"His name is Cole, and I don't think so," I replied, shaking my head. "I'd rather take my chances."

We flipped over onto our stomachs so we could get some sun on our backs. I tied my hair up into a knot on top of my head.

After a couple hours of sun, Sam and I packed up our stuff and headed into a small beachfront café for some sandwiches.

"Do you want to catch a movie tonight?" she asked as we finished up our dinner.

"Nah, I'm kind of tired. Last night I was up later than usual," I replied honestly.

"Right, kissing strangers," she brought up again. "Look, I totally get that you needed a break from everything after what had happened last summer. I get it. But I just don't want to see you miss out on an opportunity. I'm not just talking about that Cole guy, I'm talking about *anyone*."

"So you're saying I should lust after one of the guys from Soul Punch tomorrow night?" I teased. I laughed. "I'm sorry, I just can't take that stupid name seriously."

"The other guys in the band are cute too, just you wait. Maybe one of them will get you back on the horse," she countered. "Just promise me you'll think about it. Promise me that if you *do* see a guy that you could be interested in, that you'll at least give it a chance."

"I will," I groaned as we headed back to the clinic for Sam to pick up her car.

"Do you want a ride home?"

"No, I should walk. I could probably use the exercise," I replied nonchalantly. I wasn't really out of shape by any means, I had a pretty slender five-foot-seven frame. But long days at the clinic and slow afternoons at the beach didn't exactly do much for my cardio intake.

"Fine. See you tomorrow night after you get off work. I'll grab Brandt and we'll be over to your place by seven forty-five?" she said with a raised brow.

"Sounds good," I replied, waving to her as she pulled out of the lot. I thought about what she said on my walk home. Even if I did see a guy I was interested in, was I finally ready for that? Not that I had my sights on any type of band fling or something flighty like that, it wasn't my style. But clearly I wasn't going to meet anyone with something more substantial going on at a dive bar in West Cove. That's where dreams went to die.

I entered my condo and dropped my stuff, feeling more exhausted than I should for seven-thirty on a Monday. I fed all of the animals, gave them all some attention, then headed up to my bedroom for a good night's sleep. Instead of passing out right away though, my mind wandered.

There was honestly a time when I thought I would *never* be ready to date after Ian. After everything that had happened, for awhile I thought I was too love-stricken to move on. I thought giving my heart away like that to someone could only happen once in a lifetime. I figured after loving someone like that, it wasn't possible to ever feel that way again.

Shortly after that period of time though, I felt the opposite. Not love-stricken about it – but guilt-stricken.

Because deep down, I knew it was all my fault.

I was solely responsible for Ian's death.

CHAPTER 4

After a restless sleep, I awoke to a cloudy morning and a very hungry, squealing pig. I reluctantly got up, fed Dexter his breakfast, cleaned up the tortoise tank and got ready for work.

My shift at the clinic from eight to five flew by. All of the appointments were pretty routine. I missed having Sam there on Tuesdays, but she always had class on Tuesdays and Thursdays so she didn't work on those days. Eva was at least growing on me. She'd only been working at the clinic for about eight months. She was a little bit older, in her late thirties, and she was unmarried. Aside from her soap opera obsession, she loved parakeets more than any other bird lover I'd ever met. We didn't necessarily have a lot in common, but she had a great sense of humor and was fun to be around.

"So, any details for me on the hunk from the other night?" she questioned as I sorted through some charts towards the end of my shift. "Possibly a date tonight?"

"Nope, no juicy details for you," I said wearily. These people see me leave one time with a guy and they can't let it go. "I'm headed out tonight with Sam for a concert. It's at some dive bar in West Cove though, so if I don't show up for work tomorrow, somebody needs to come look for my body."

"Those West Cove boys would enjoy doing something to your body, all right," she said with animated eyebrows. "You watch out tonight. See, that's why you need that hunk of a man, to take care of you in a place like that."

"Brandt is going with us, we'll be fine," I stated, setting down the charts and grabbing for my purse.

"That skinny little friend of yours that comes in here for lunch sometimes? He's going to save you?" she asked with a laugh.

"I'm not the one who will need saving. Sam is going nuts for some guy in a crappy band. Who knows how the night will end," I said, only half sarcastically. Sam didn't always have the best taste when it came to dating material. They were always cute, but sometimes had little else to offer.

I said my goodbyes and made the short walk back to my condo. I took a quick shower and dried my long hair, opting to keep it down for the night. I tried to pick out something dive-bar-concert-worthy, but I had no clue what this place was really like. Sam and Brandt rang my doorbell just a few minutes before eight.

"You're wearing pants?" Sam asked me with a scrunched up face as I answered the door. I guessed by her tight black dress that she expected me in something different.

"I don't know, I'm just trying stuff on," I said in a frustrated tone, throwing up my hands. "I don't usually frequent seedy bars on the wrong side of town. I feel like I'm suppose to wear leather or metal or something."

"You're not a biker chick for heaven's sake," Sam said, leading me back upstairs to my closet. Brandt just shrugged at me in his khaki pants and light green button down shirt as we left him in the living room. "We're going to flirt with hot guys in a band," she said, rummaging through my hangers. "You need something tighter… Shorter."

"You're the one flirting with band guys," I said with a laugh. "I'll be hanging out with Brandt in the back corner of the bar trying not to get mugged. I've never heard anything good about the bars in West Cove, other than they're fabulous places to score cheap heroin."

"That's why Brandt is with us, for security so no one takes advantage of us," Sam further explained, holding out a short navy and white striped sundress. "This doesn't look all that daring, but it's the shortest thing you've got. You're my wingman. Please wear this instead of the pants?" she pled. Her giant hazel eyes begged.

"Whatever," I said, shooing her out. "Give me two minutes." I heard her tall heels thump down the stairs as I slid the strapless dress over my head. It was at least longer than the dress Sam had on, but not by much.

I only had on light makeup, versus the black eyeliner and smoky eyes Sam had, but I felt comfortable. After all, I was just going as the supportive friend, so I didn't want to overdo it. The least amount of attention I could bring to myself, the better. I grabbed a small clutch purse with my ID and very little cash and ran downstairs to head out. Brandt was currently on the floor, scratching Dexter's tummy, while Sam was fixing her makeup in my hallway mirror.

"This pig is amazing," Brandt said, playing with his snout. "How much longer do you have him?"

"Only until Friday," I said sadly. "Nikki found a home for him."

"Maybe someday you'll focus less on real pigs and you'll find yourself a human one instead," Sam teased.

"A girl can dream," I said with a laugh. "Dexter, here," I insisted, pointing to the baby gate area he stayed in with a litter box while I was away. He followed my command and stepped right in. "This one is at least listening to me," I stated with a smirk. "I'd rather have a pig."

I shut off a few lights and we headed out for the night, climbing into Brandt's yellow Hummer.

"Does this band play anywhere other than West Cove bars?" he asked Sam as he drove us towards the locale. "I'm afraid we're all going to end up on the news tomorrow. Look at this place."

I gazed out my window, taking in the liquor stores with barred windows. There was a lady on the other side of the street looking disheveled while pushing around an empty shopping cart. There was good reason why we stayed around downtown Mountain Ridge. This definitely wasn't our scene.

"According to their website, their next three gigs are at Local Joes, so this is our only option," Sam sighed. "But I promise you Syd, when you see this guy it will all make sense. I would do the same for you."

"I know you would," I replied earnestly. Sam was one of the best people I knew, so of course I didn't mind joining her for this adventure. She would do it for me without hesitation.

"What's his name?" Brandt asked, following his GPS instructions down an unlit side street.

"Here we go," I teased. "It's either Luke or Ethan or Barry."

"Or Tyler," Sam interjected. "I know, it's embarrassing. But I love you both for being here with me," she said sincerely. "This is it." She pointed to a small blue building. There was a jankity sign out front that read *Local Joe's*. The wood siding was peeling off and two of the parking lot lights appeared to be burnt out. *Lovely.*

"There are a decent amount of cars here for a Tuesday night," Brandt said, pulling into one of the few vacant spots left.

"May we all live not to regret this," I teased as we climbed out of the SUV. A few heads turned our way in the parking lot. Turns out we weren't blending in as well as we'd hoped, but I blamed Brandt's loud attention seeking car for that.

Brandt held out some bills to the bouncer checking IDs, covering our five dollar entrance fee. The place inside was bigger than I expected. There was a long bar area with people lining up for drinks, and a few tables set up towards the back of the room with chairs. There was a decent-sized stage full of instruments with a somewhat sad homemade drop cloth hung up baring the words *Soul Punch*. I snickered again at the name. It was so dumb.

"The usuals?" Brandt asked towards Sam and I, pointing to the bar. We both nodded. Sam was scouring the room for any sign of her band target. Within a minute, the room went completely dark.

"Dammit, we really are going to be murdered here," I muttered, grabbing onto Sam's arm in the dark. Seconds later a small spotlight turned on, illuminating the stage.

"That scared the piss out of me," Brandt said, walking up behind us. "I spilled Sam's cranberry vodka all over myself." Brandt looked annoyed as he handed us our drinks. He wiped his clothes down with a bar napkin.

A loud voice came over the speakers, introducing the band. Immediately following that were drums so loud I could barely hear the vocals. Sam grabbed my arm, pointing to the guitarist. He had on dark jeans and a grey tank top, and his brown messy hair looked chaotic. He was so into the music though, it was as if he didn't even realize how many people were looking at him.

"He's cute," I shouted to Sam over the music. She stared at him all googly-eyed, sipping on her cranberry vodka.

"Please come with me to talk to him after the show," she pled.

"I can't imagine risking my life here to leave empty-handed," I agreed. I never would've approached a guy for myself, but it was easy for me to do for a friend. There was no pressure.

I glanced around the room. It was a diverse crowd, that was for sure. There were a lot of young girls who looked underage. They were wearing too much makeup, probably in order to help them pass with their fake IDs. There were also groups of guys, most of them full of piercings and tattoos, and some couples awkwardly trying to dance to the hard rock music. I definitely didn't see anyone else like us around.

The band played four or five more songs in a row. Sam was right, the music wasn't great, but it was tolerable. The guitarist guy she was ogling looked really into it, but a couple of the other guys in the band looked like they were really overdoing it. The band finally announced a brief intermission and jumped off the stage where they headed to the bar for some shots.

"Do you want to talk to him now?" I asked Sam, trying to read the expression on her face.

"I can't, I'm too nervous," she said excitedly. "Can we just wait until after the show?"

"That's fine," I nodded, finishing up my drink. Sam's glass was also already empty.

"Some giant security guy is staring at you, Syd. He looks questionable. I swear he is wearing what appears to be a shirt from the Baby Gap," Brandt said, gesturing towards the bar area. "He's huge. He's been staring at you for at least five minutes."

I narrowed my eyes towards the bar area, trying to see who he was talking about. Was that… *Cole*?

The guy across the room nodded as soon as I made eye contact with him, confirming I was right. "Oh my gosh, I know him. That's the guy from the clinic the other night," I explained to Sam. "Give me a minute."

I walked towards Cole and he walked towards me, meeting each other right in between the bar area and the main room.

"How did you know I would be here?" he asked with a smirk and a raised brow. "I left you my number, you could've just called."

"I was just about to ask if you're following me," I countered. "What are you doing here?" He couldn't have possibly known I would be in this bar tonight.

"Tyler, the bassist, is a buddy of mine. We come to all his shows," he replied, staring at me curiously. "You really didn't know I was here? Are you telling me this is a completely random encounter? Like a cute story you could tell your friends about how we met?" he asked, referencing our conversation from the other night. He smirked at me, waiting for my reply.

"I guess it is," I stated, mildly amused. It was awfully coincidental to run into him again.

"So then we can start over, like we don't know each other then," he said casually, shrugging his shoulders. "I can ask you out now like you've never turned me down, right?" His eyes lit up as he said it. "I'm Cole Mason, nice to meet you in this random, yet insanely romantic spot. I love unexpected meetings like this," he teased.

I laughed. "I'm Sydney Summers, pleasure to meet you. What did you do to your arm there?" I asked, playing his game. "That looks like quite an injury."

"Yeah, it's nothing really. I think I was just rescuing a helpless kitten from a burning tree. Something like that. I'm always doing things like that, saving animals and stuff. I'm really into that kind of thing."

I laughed again, amused by his sense of humor.

"Does this mean you'll go get tacos with me now? It's like the universe is practically forcing us together, right?" he said playfully. "It doesn't have to be a date, I didn't mean to add any pressure to it like that. It can be more like a 'thanks for fixing my arm so I don't get sepsis' kind of dinner. We can sit around talking about the awesome soul-crushing melodies of Soul Punch."

I let out a slight giggle. The more I heard the band name, the more it was growing on me in a funny, ironic way. The stupidity of it somehow brought me joy every time someone said it, simply because it was *that* bad. I thought back to my conversation with Sam yesterday, when she begged me to just give some guy a chance. *Any* guy. I promised her I would, more in an effort to get her off my back, but this seemed like a better idea than finding another guy in the crowd to try it out on.

"I would love to go eat tacos with you Cole Mason," I replied. He smiled at me and it was infectious.

"Is tomorrow night too long for you to wait? Because we could probably get there before they close at nine if you want to rush me into it," he said sarcastically.

"Tomorrow would be perfect," I responded.

"Just out of curiosity, what are you actually doing here? This isn't the safest place for a girl like you," he said sincerely.

"I picked up on that," I replied, looking around. "But my friend Sam is crushing on the guitarist so I told her I would wingman for her tonight. We did bring Brandt with us though, for added protection."

Cole looked around me to where Brandt and Sam were standing, pretending not to be watching us. "You're telling me the guy with juice all over his khakis is your security for the night?"

I snickered as he said it.

"Please tell me you wouldn't leave here with anyone," he said protectively. "I mean, I know you're confident with your karate, but these guys here, they aren't good guys."

"You know all of them?" I asked skeptically.

"Pretty much," he replied, looking around the room. "Which guy does she like, Luke? The guitar guy?"

I nodded. "Yeah. He doesn't look too scary."

"Oh no," he said, shaking his head. "You are too naïve to be in here. Please don't be offended by that, but I'm serious. These guys here aren't your friends, and they don't want to be. I don't know Luke all that well, but I know who he hangs around well enough to know that your friend shouldn't be alone with them."

"That's why I'm here with her, she won't be alone. We can handle it."

"I'm not phrasing this right," he said, trying to gather his thoughts. "I don't want to sound possessive, or jealous, or crazy or anything, but I'm serious. You guys shouldn't be here. And you absolutely cannot leave with any of these guys. Will Brandt at least stay with you guys the whole night?"

"He will," I said, appreciating the concern in his voice. "We're not going anywhere tonight. She just wants to meet him. Maybe they can plan something for another time?"

"Can I intervene? What day does she want to make plans with him?" he asked.

"Well, we work tomorrow and Friday, and she has class on Thursday. Maybe Saturday?" I guessed.

"If I promise to make it happen will you promise me you'll leave after the show?"

"Yes," I said hesitantly. Now he just seemed to be a bit overprotective. I wondered if he thought I was interested in someone else, or if he was really as concerned as he pretended to be.

"Luke," Cole called over to the bar. The guitarist came over and they did some weird 'bro shake' - part fist-bumping, part hand shaking.

He led Luke over to where Sam and Brandt were standing. "I want you to meet my friends, this is Sam," he said, directing Luke's attention to my beaming friend.

"I love your music, you are very talented," she gushed. He smiled and reached out for her hand, kissing it as she outstretched it. I wasn't sure if the gesture was sincere or slimy.

"Well thank you," Luke said kindly, still keeping his eyes on Sam. They definitely liked looking at each other. I don't think they broke eye contact.

"So Sydney and I were thinking about taking the boat out on Saturday, do you want to join us?" Cole suggested. Sam looked from Cole to me, wondering how on earth all of this just happened. I loved the way he simultaneously made plans for me and him at the same time – very clever. But because it was helping out Sam, I didn't mind one bit.

"I'd love to," Luke replied. "How do you guys know each other?" he asked, looking from Cole to the three of us.

"Syd and I watch baseball together sometimes," Cole replied, subtly winking at me. "Sam and Brandt are good friend of hers. You can join us too if you'd like Brandt," he added sincerely.

"Thanks man, but I have to work on Saturday," he uttered, picking up on the whole double date vibe. Brandt looked to me for confirmation that he answered that correctly. I smiled at him.

"Hey, I gotta get back on stage," Luke said, pointing to his band mates walking towards their instruments. "Looking forward to Saturday though. Cole, you'll text me the details?"

"Yeah, man, we'll talk after the show. Get back at it," Cole said, motioning him to head back to his band.

"Nice to meet you," Luke said, walking away backwards towards the stage, still maintaining eye contact with Sam.

As soon as he was out of earshot, Sam exploded. "Syd, I think I love this guy," she gushed, pointing towards Cole. "Are we really going on a boat Saturday?" She was so excited.

"Yep, Sydney practically begged me," he said sarcastically, "so I had to make it happen. What time do you guys want to head out? Around two that afternoon?"

"That works, we both have the day off," Sam replied, grinning from ear to ear.

"Do you guys want another drink?" Cole asked us politely. "What is that, a cranberry vodka? A sea breeze? It's something pink, I can see that."

"None of those," I replied with a soft laugh. "I'm fine, really. I don't need anything else."

"I will take you up on a cranberry vodka though," Sam chimed in. "My nerves are all revved up, I think I need it." Cole and Brandt left us briefly to head to the bar for the refills.

"That's the guy from the clinic?" Sam gushed a little too loudly as they walked away. "How are you in limbo as to whether or not you should be seeing that guy? You should be seeing *every* bit of that guy, oh my gosh. That whole package…"

"I don't even know him," I interrupted. "Get over his handsome face for Pete's sake, he could be a violent criminal or something."

"That's all something I could look past for a guy like that," she teased.

I playfully rolled my eyes at her. "If I was into a guy with muscles, I would just go hang out at a gym somewhere. That's not what I'm about."

"How are you my best friend?" she teased back.

Seconds later the band started back up and it was too loud for any more conversation. Brandt and Cole returned, handing Sam her drink. Cole stood right next to me and looked down on me, smiling, and I felt a lot more comfortable in the room than I had minutes earlier. Any uncomfortable feelings I had about the place were completely washed away with him standing by my side.

The band played another five songs, none of them really sticking out to me. They all sounded kind of the same. When it was over, Cole grabbed my hand and squeezed it gently. "I need to talk to someone real quick. Will you hang around for a minute? I don't want you to leave yet." I nodded. Sam's smile grew immensely as Luke hopped off the stage and made his way towards her.

"I only have a minute. The next band is up in a few and they're real jerks if we don't get our stuff cleared out quickly," he explained. "But what are you guys up to tonight? Do you guys want to hang? We can head out of here with some of my friends."

"We have to work pretty early tomorrow," I interjected. If I'd left the response up to Sam, she would have agreed with anything he asked of her. I could see it in her eyes. "We have to head out. But great show, that was fun. We'll see you on Saturday?"

"Yeah, looking forward to it," he stated. As soon as Luke walked away, two more guys approached us. So much for Brandt warning them away. These guys didn't even acknowledge he was standing with us.

"Haven't seen you around here before," one of them snarled. "Are you ladies sticking around, or do you want to head to a party with us?"

"On a Tuesday night? Who has a party on a Tuesday?" Brandt chimed in. They completely ignored him.

"We've got some goods out in the Camero," the other guy said with a lip full of chew. "Interested?"

"That's the pickup line around here? You're inviting us out to your Camero?" I said in sarcastic disbelief. "We're good, but thanks."

"Don't be disrespecting my car, sweetheart," the guy growled. "Otherwise I'd be happy to bend you over the hood for a good spanking."

"Yeah, I'm not four years old, so we're good," I replied, grabbing Sam's hand. "We should head out."

Brandt turned to head out of the bar. We were only two steps behind him, but in that amount of time, another burly guy in a Def Leppard shirt with the sleeves ripped off stepped in front of us.

"You ladies look like a good time," he said with a sleazy look on his face. "Don't be thinking you're just gonna leave here without having some conversation with us first." Two more guys came up and stood next to him.

"She knows karate, back off," a booming voice said behind us. I smirked, obviously realizing it was Cole. The guys simply looked up at Cole in disgust, not saying anything further. Brandt turned around to see the commotion, stopping in his tracks. He didn't seem sure as to whether or not he was supposed to intervene.

Brandt reached back and grabbed Sam's hand. Cole wrapped an arm around my shoulder. The men in front of us moved, and we walked out of the bar.

"See what I mean?" he said towards me. "These guys are animals."

"What about you? You're here," I retorted.

"Only to save innocent girls like you from very bad things," he said under his breath. "Can I please take you home?" Brandt and Sam were already making their way towards the Hummer.

"I rode with them, they'll take me back," I said with a shrug. "We're fine. We're heading home."

"Tell Brandt to make sure no one is following you," he said sternly.

"Why would someone follow us? I think you might be blowing this out of proportion," I began, not understanding why he was so adamant about how bad these people were. Sure, the guys were mostly dirty and appeared to have some ill intentions, but they weren't exactly physical with us. I didn't feel all that uncomfortable.

"Please," he urged. "Just trust me on this."

I stared up into his eyes, trying to read them. They didn't look possessive or jealous or demanding. They looked full of genuine concern.

"Would it make you feel better to follow us back?" I offered.

"Yes," he replied, sounding relieved. He walked me to Brandt's Hummer and opened the door for me. "Nice meeting you guys," he said towards Brandt and Sam up front. "See you Saturday Sam."

"I still can't believe we're going out," she said dreamily. She was on cloud nine.

"I'll follow you," he said softly.

I put on my seatbelt and he closed the door. Brandt pulled out of the parking lot and I smiled as I heard the soft hum of a motorcycle behind us.

"I still can't believe that was Cole," Sam said with a disbelieving tone. "What about that guy isn't your type? That face… those arms… and he has a boat?" she added excitedly. "Please, Syd, please go out with him. That's the last thing I'll ever beg of you."

"We're going out tomorrow night," I said with a sigh.

"Eeek!" Sam screamed. "This is major. We should go celebrate."

"Let's see if I even make it through dinner with him. I'm pretty out of practice. I haven't been on a first date in years." Ian and I were together for two, and that was over a year ago. I was seriously unprepared for this. "Besides, we can't go anywhere else, or I can't go with you anyway. He's following me back to my place."

Brandt's eyes darted up to his rearview mirror and Sam looked in her side mirror simultaneously.

"He's going back to your place tonight?" she shrieked. She was way too excited about all of this. "So that's why you didn't want us to make plans with Luke tonight, I get it."

"No, that's not it at all. He's just making sure we get back safely, that's it," I corrected her. "He seemed worried about it. Like someone would follow us or something. I don't know, it was kind of strange, but kind of sweet all at the same time."

"I am staying up all night until you call me with the details," Sam threatened as we pulled up my street. "I'm serious, I don't care what time it is, you have to call me."

"He's literally just making sure I'm home okay. That's it. Don't stay up."

"Call me if anything happens," she reiterated as Brandt pulled up in front of my door.

I thanked Brandt for driving us and waved goodbye. Cole's motorcycle pulled forward in front of my place as soon as Brandt began pulling out.

I walked towards him and he shut off the engine. He climbed off the bike and walked towards me.

"Can I walk you up?" he said, pointing towards the small path and four steps I had to walk. It seemed silly in a way given how short of a distance it was, but it was also sweet.

"Of course," I agreed. "Thanks for the escort tonight. Do you want to come in?"

"Yes," he said quietly, staring at me with an intense gaze. It burned through me and I so badly wanted his lips against mine again. "I want to. But I can't. Not tonight." He reached out and brushed the hair back from my face. As his fingers grazed my skin, I felt it pulse through my entire body.

"You won't come in?" I clarified, a little surprised by his reply.

"Then you'll think me following you home was probably just some ploy to spend more time with you," he said softly. "I feel like I need to walk away so you truly understand that my intentions were just to get you home safely. That's all I meant to do."

"If you're telling me that, I believe you," I replied, studying his face.

"I don't want to scare you, but those guys there tonight, guys from West Cove… They're dangerous, Sydney. I don't want them around you."

"Well I have no plans on heading back there," I said with a soft laugh, trying to lighten the mood. "It was just for Sam."

"You guys won't be heading back there for any more shows?" he asked with a serious tone to his voice.

"No," I said skeptically. "But why the dramatics? I get it, there are probably some sleazy guys there who wouldn't mind harming us, but following me home? Why would they want to go out of their way to hurt me?"

"That's the thing, it's not you," he said, shaking his head. "They want to hurt *me*."

CHAPTER 5

Cole said goodnight to me somewhat abruptly, insisting again that he didn't want to come in so that I wouldn't misread his intentions. Quite honestly, I wasn't sure what his ultimate intentions were. He simply said he'd pick me up after work around seven to go out for tacos and that was the end of it. He watched me walk inside, got on his motorcycle and rode away.

My night of sleep was interrupted by weird dreams. West Cove either appeared completely corrupt and terrible in my head, or sometimes in my dreams it would appear like the happiest place on earth, with rainbows overhead and cute puppy dogs roaming the well-kept front yards of sweet-looking houses. Cole never appeared in any of my dreams, but some other unsavory men did.

I made it into work just before six a.m., and I was happy it was a day Sam was there. The hours passed by so much quicker when we had the same shift. She was no doubt disappointed that I had no story with Cole the night before, but I assured her I would have *something* to tell her about our date tonight, good or bad.

I mindlessly performed numerous x-rays, took urine samples, and assisted Dr. Nikki in a few minor surgeries. Finally three o'clock rolled around.

"Do you want to head to the beach for a bit?" Sam asked, trying to gauge how I felt about any plans before my date tonight.

"Sure," I agreed, figuring a little normal downtime would be beneficial. My nerves started to creep up into my throat. I didn't even know what I was nervous about – other than *everything*.

Sam drove us back to my place after our shift and we fed the pig and the tortoise, then grabbed our beach bags. She kept one at my house since we typically left from there anyway. It was easier than her carting it to work every day.

While we were lying in the sun, she asked a couple times if I wanted to talk about anything, but I declined. I didn't want to think about the date before I had to.

Finally a little after five we packed up our stuff and headed back to the condo.

"If you need anything, call me," Sam said sincerely. "But remember, you promised me you'd give this a chance."

"Get out of here," I said with a laugh. "No pep talk. I'll call you later. Or, since you don't work tomorrow, I'll keep you waiting in great suspense until I see you on Friday."

"You would never be so cruel," she shouted back as she climbed into her car.

I took a long shower and the warm water rejuvenated me. What was I going to wear tonight? He did drive a motorcycle. Any type of dress or skirt was out if I was going to be straddling him. Geez, a first date and my legs were already going to be wrapped around him. No wonder guys loved motorcycles.

I dried my thick hair and scrunched it up a bit, keeping it simple with my natural wave. I grabbed a hair tie for my wrist, expecting to tie it all up anyway as soon as we got on his bike.

It's just tacos. I had to remind myself that this was just a simple, casual dinner. Nothing fancy. I put on some tight dark jeans and a cute white blousy shirt. It was a simple outfit, but still very feminine without showing any leg. I wore a high pair of wedge sandals. I loved how tall Cole was. I didn't have to even consider my flats like I always did with Ian, since he was only two inches taller than me. The sun was about to start its descent behind the mountain tops, which meant the air would cool considerably by the time he picked me up, so the jeans felt like a good choice.

A few minutes before seven, there was a soft knock on my front door. I gave Dexter a quick chin scratch and said goodbye, grabbing my purse and a light sweatshirt as I opened the door.

"Very prompt," I said with a smile as I made eye contact with him. He was wearing dark jeans and a white collared shirt with the sleeves rolled up halfway. I was surprised to see him in flip flops. Although I wasn't sure what I really expected – motorcycle boots? Was that even a thing? What shoes did he have on last night? I hadn't even noticed.

"Harvey taught me to never make a woman wait. Whoa, we practically match," he said with a smirk, pointing to my outfit. "Next time we should really coordinate this better." He spoke so jovially that despite the butterflies in my stomach, he put me at ease. I noticed a large black truck parked in front of my house.

"I brought the truck instead of the bike for tonight," he said, picking up on my gaze. "I wasn't sure how you felt about the motorcycle, so I figured that could wait." His thoughtfulness floored me. Quite honestly, motorcycles terrified me, but I wouldn't have said a word about it if that was our transportation tonight. The fact that he genuinely thought about it ahead of time was extremely courteous. "If you're disappointed, we can go back for the bike," he added, trying to read my expression.

"No, this is perfect," I said warmly. I threw my sweatshirt back on the couch as I turned out the lights and locked my front door. "I forgot to mention it last night, but thanks for the towels the other day. You didn't have to do that."

"Hey, when I bleed all over a woman's linens I replace them. It's just the kind of guy I am," he joked. "And tacos. They're my ultimate groveling gift. Whether I'm thankful, or apologetic, or begging for something… tacos are my answer. So I hope you really know how appreciative I am of you fixing up my arm."

He helped me into the cab of his truck, which was lifted pretty high. The inside was impeccable – not a single crumb or piece of paper. It felt brand new.

He climbed into the truck and started up the engine, smiling at me from the driver's seat. "Have you ever been to Antonio's before?" he asked with a raised brow.

"I don't think so," I commented. Most of the restaurants I ever went to were in downtown Mountain Ridge. Cole was headed towards the other side of the lake. "It sounds Italian."

"That's the beauty of this place," he said excitedly, "Antonio, the owner, *is* an Italian guy. But he's obsessed with tacos. So he opened up this little dive and he only makes Mexican food. The place itself isn't all that great, but there are some tables across from there near the beach. It's one of my favorite spots."

"Sounds wonderful," I commented, looking forward to trying something new. We continued driving west for a few minutes before finally pulling off the main road.

"This is it," he said with a huge grin, maneuvering his truck into a small lot in front of a tiny yellow building. "Like I said, the inside isn't much, but we'll sit over there." He pointed to an area of picnic tables across the street from where we parked. They faced a beautiful little stretch of beach. The water looked perfectly calm tonight, and a few stars began appearing overhead as the sun began to slip past the horizon.

We climbed out of his truck and he led me into the restaurant, holding the door open as I passed through. A small menu board hung above the counter. A petite dark-haired guy who looked to be in his forties smiled as soon as he saw us.

"Antonio," Cole said happily. The two men did a pseudo handshake similar to the one I saw Cole exchange last night with Luke. It was definitely some weird version of male communication.

"I haven't seen you for at least a week," Antonio said with animated arms. "I was beginning to think you left me for tacos cooked by a Mexican. Now I see you just found something better than tacos altogether," he said, slightly nodding towards me.

"I've been busy at the shop, Harvey had a bit of a setback," Cole answered vaguely. "This is Sydney. She helped me out of a bind," Cole stated, holding up his still-wrapped left forearm.

"This guy is all muscles but it takes a pretty girl to save him from trouble," Antonio teased. "What'll it be tonight?"

"Do you mind if I order for you?" Cole asked politely. "You've gotta try a bunch of these to know what you really like here."

I smiled and nodded at him. "Sure, I eat pretty much anything. Just not too spicy."

"One of each from the left side, please," Cole relayed to Antonio.

"Oh Syndey, you found yourself a man who knows how to properly treat a woman," Antonio replied with his Italian accent and a smile.

Cole held out some money towards Antonio, but he shook his head and refused.

"Your money is no good tonight," he stated, still shaking his head. "You brought me a new lifelong customer. I shall thank you for that with tacos."

"See, I'm not the only one who says thank you with tacos," Cole said to me. Antonio headed towards the back of the restaurant and within three or four minutes he came out with a heaping tray of wrapped food. "Thanks man, I appreciate it," Cole said as he grabbed the tray.

"Besides, I'll be taking your money tomorrow night for cards, yes?" Antonio asked as we made our way out of the restaurant. We filled up the two empty paper cups he gave us at the soda machine.

"Yep, I'll be there," Cole said over his shoulder. He held the door open for me again and we made our way out of the small building. We headed across the street to the beach area he pointed to earlier.

Cole laid the food out and joined me on the same side of the table. "I know this feels like a trick so I can sit close to you, but I swear I'm just in this for the view."

I smiled shyly and looked at him as he sat down next to me. His arms and chest pressed tightly against his form fitting white shirt. His smile looked warm on his tan face and his light brown hair was short on the sides and perfectly combed on top. He looked like a guy you'd see in a beer commercial – tan and strong and slightly rugged – but yet with such a sincere smile that warmed his eyes and made you want to party with him.

"If these aren't the best tacos you've ever had, we probably can't be friends," he stated, unwrapping the food. "So please, think about your reaction to them before you speak. Because I think we definitely need to be friends."

"Oh yeah?" I replied with an amused laugh. "What makes you think I'm even a good friend? I might be the type to borrow your clothes without asking, or maybe I'll talk about you to all my other friends when you're not around."

"You have my full permission to borrow my clothes any time you want," he teased back. "And I should be so lucky for you to talk about me to your friends."

I narrowed my eyes at him, trying to figure him out. He was witty and fun and charismatic. Part of me found it odd that I'd never seen him around before in such a relatively small town, but then part of me wondered how it came to be that we really met each other at all, given how different we seemed.

"So what's your story? Are you from Mountain Ridge?" I inquired, changing our conversation. I really didn't know a lot about him, other than the fact he drove a motorcycle and he said Harvey was his father. When I went out on dates back in college, I felt like I knew them first before it got to that point. Other than two random run-ins with this guy, he was still essentially a stranger.

"Yep, born and raised all twenty-four years of my life," he answered, handing me a taco. "I'll spare you the boring details, but Harvey has pretty much raised me since I was twelve. I work for him, and also at a shop fixing up bikes on the side."

"What exactly do you do for Harvey?" I asked, curious to know more.

"A little bit of everything," he replied with a shrug. "I run a lot of errands for him, stuff like that. He gives me a free place to stay in a cabin behind his, plus a decent cut of his business for the week."

"What exactly is Harvey's business?" I further asked, taking a bite of my taco. Cole was right, the flavors were delectable. I tasted seasoned steak strips, lettuce, and some kind of fruit salsa. It was absolutely amazing.

"Nothing interesting," he replied nonchalantly. "Let's just say it's not your typical nine to five. There's a lot of money changing hands, that kind of thing. Honestly he keeps me out of the loop on most of it. I'm just in charge of drop-offs and pick-ups. I go where he tells me and follow his orders. That's about it."

I was pretty sure there was more to it. Surely Cole knew more about what he was doing for Harvey, especially if he'd been close to him all these years. I didn't want to push the questions though. He didn't seem to want to elaborate.

"It's all temporary though," Cole added, continuing the conversation. "I doubt I'll live here too much longer."

"Where are you going?" I questioned, polishing off my first taco.

"Hopefully southern California," he said with a shrug, as if his plan wasn't fully solidified yet. "I have some ideas, but if there's one thing I've learned in my life, I know plans are fluid. I know everything can change in a single instant. So, I'm planning on it and we'll see when it happens."

He stared directly into my eyes as he said it. His words resonated with me more than he realized. My life had been a pretty simple one for the most part, but unfortunately I also realized in an instant how cruel the world could be. How life-altering it could be in a single split second. There was no way to plan for that.

"I understand what you mean," I commiserated.

"So what about you, what are your life plans?" he asked sincerely.

"To finish the rest of these tacos," I teased. "You were right, I've never had Mexican food like this. It's amazing."

"Well it's official then, we can be friends," he stated with a soft laugh. "But after the tacos, what's your plan then?"

I hesitated for a moment. The first thought that entered my mind was that I wondered what his chest looked like without his shirt. I almost wanted to reach out and put my hand on his chest, just to see if it really felt as rock hard as it appeared through the thin fabric. Then I immediately chided myself for those thoughts. *Get it together, Syd.* In what world did my future plans include undressing handsome strangers?

"My life plans have changed a lot," I stated honestly. "I graduated in May and here I am, not really sure what I'm doing."

"What was your plan originally?" he asked, handing me another taco.

"Well, this summer I was supposed to be moving to Washington State to start my graduate program in the fall," I began, not sure of how much to tell him. The full story wasn't exactly first date worthy. Quite honestly, I would've been happy to never talk about it again. "But I've officially turned that opportunity down," I said vaguely. "Sam is still heading out to Oregon though next month and I'll still be here. So I guess I need a new plan."

"Sweet. Then why don't you move to southern California with me? We'll start a taco stand," he joked.

"That sounds about as random as what I have in mind," I replied, trying the second taco. This one was full of chicken and avocados with some sort of tangy sauce. It tasted even better than the first one.

"These other two are spicy," he explained, completely shifting the conversation. I was relieved by that. I certainly wanted to know more about him, but I can't say I was all that eager to tell him more about myself. "Do you want to at least try them?"

I nodded and he held one out to me. I bit into it, trying to decipher all of the flavors. This one tasted like shredded pork. He was right though, the spicy pepper sauce on it certainly had a kick.

"It's good, but hot," I commented once I swallowed the bite.

"Try this one."

I took a quick sip of my Sprite before biting into the next taco he held up. I couldn't even figure out what was in that one – different meats, some crazy type of chunky salsa. It was pretty fiery.

"That one's too much for me," I said, quickly taking a sip of my drink.

"I'm impressed you bit into it without even knowing what they were," he stated with a raised brow. "It's quickly changing my opinion of you." He had a boyish grin and I couldn't help but smile back at him.

"Do I even want to know what your opinion is?" I mused.

"Not until I have you figured out. I need more time. You're an enigma. You're all pretty and proper one minute, then you're dive-bar hopping and eating taco stand food the next. You're all over the place, I can't quite get an accurate read on you. You have a pig living in your kitchen, but yet you have no hesitation finishing off a pork taco. You're fascinating."

I wasn't sure if he was completely mocking me, but his tone was sweet. Honestly I couldn't figure him out either, so we had that in common.

"Do all the other girls turn down your tacos when you shove them in front of their mouths?" I said lightheartedly.

"You're the first girl I've ever brought here actually," he said sweetly. "Usually I just hang around here trying to pick up on ones who already share my love of Tony's," he teased.

I playfully swatted his arm. "Well while we're on the subject, where's your girlfriend? Or did you dump her because she was a vegetarian or something?" I joked.

“No girl,” he replied. “Not for a long time.”

“I imagine your strong stature and perfect jaw line are quite a turn off for most women,” I said sarcastically.

“So you noticed my face,” he replied playfully. “Everyone else just stares at my chest. I know what you women go through. The struggle is real.”

I laughed as he said it, appreciating his sense of humor. I enjoyed being around him even more than I thought I would. For some reason I thought our dinner might be quiet and awkward, or that I would be so nervous that I would start rambling about baseball again, or something else just as stupid. Instead though, I felt perfectly comfortable to be with him.

“I’m sure you have to work early tomorrow, but can we walk down by the beach? I want to show you something,” he asked.

“Tomorrow is actually my late start day,” I replied. “I don’t go in until nine. I don’t have to be home that early.” *Eeek.* An omission that I wouldn’t mind staying out late with him. I hoped the way I said it sounded more casual than eager.

“Stay here,” he instructed, gathering up our trash. He ran the tray back across the street to Antonio’s and came back to meet me at the table.

“How’s your arm by the way?” I asked, finally able to direct my attention to the real reason why we were here. After all, I did promise him the night we met that I would look at it again for him. "Did you unwrap it yet? Any redness?"

"It's fine," he said with a dismissive shrug. "I've had worse."

"Worse than a stab wound? Who are you, Cole Mason?"

"Like you've never been stabbed before," he said in a mocking tone.

I laughed. "Are you going to tell me what really happened?" I studied his face as he reached out his hand for mine. I grabbed it and he led me towards the beach, not letting go of my grasp. We kicked our shoes off and I was reminded just how short I was next to him without my heels on. The sand felt cold on my bare feet.

"I will eventually," he replied with a smirk. "I'll tell you what, I know we're going out on the boat Saturday, but Friday night my friends are having a bonfire on the beach. If you aren't terrified that's too much time to spend with me, will you go with me? It doesn't start until nine, but after midnight, that's when all my secrets come out." His smile was so contagious that I couldn't help but smile back.

"That sounds fun actually," I answered sincerely. I wondered if we knew any of the same people or if it would be a totally new crowd. Maybe some of the same people from the bar last night? Then again, I didn't see him hanging around a particular group of people. Once we spotted each other, he didn't seem to talk to anyone else.

"Look over by these rocks," he said, leading me over to a rougher part of the shoreline. We stepped over some large rocks that were partially in the water. He pointed to a small clearing in the sand. There were weird indentations in the tide. "This is the best place to see the turtles hatching," he explained, exploring around by the rocks. "See these patterns in the sand here?" he pointed. "This is the spot. Usually this is the best time of night for it. See all those eggs there?"

"How on earth do you know this exists?" I said excitedly.

"I've been coming here for years, ever since I was a kid. I don't live too far from here," he said innocently. "I stumbled upon this spot once, just walking around after dark. Once you see it, you'll be hooked. Then again, you've probably seen it before, given your profession."

"Never," I replied, feeling giddy over the possibility of it. I'd seen documentaries about it, sure. But never the real thing.

"You might be mad at me for this, but I think it's a false alarm. I don't see any movement," he confessed, gently moving some of the rocks around. "I'm guessing it won't happen until tomorrow night."

"Can we come back?" I said eagerly. "Please? I have to see it. Please?"

"Yes, I'll go out with you again. Geez, you're so persistent," he teased.

"This is for the turtles," I clarified humorously.

"Right," he said with a fake disbelieving tone.

"I have to work until seven tomorrow night. Don't you have cards or something?" I asked, remembering Antonio's comment earlier. "Pinochle? Bridge?"

"It's poker, but I can be late," he said with a boyish grin. "We do it every month. It's no big deal if I get a late start. Do you want me to pick you up?"

"Yes!" I said excitedly. "Is seven fifteen too late? That way I can go home and change real quick after work. Will we miss it?"

"Nah, that should be perfect timing," he said thoughtfully. He grabbed my hand again and we headed back down the beach towards his truck.

"Are you going to let me look at your arm tonight?" I asked, genuinely concerned about it. I wasn't entirely confident I bandaged it up well enough in the first place. Not to mention there was a part of me that wanted to extend our evening beyond just dinner.

"That would be great," he replied politely, still keeping a firm grip on my hand as he led me back across the street to his truck. "First let's go somewhere else. You don't seem like a drinker, so a bar is probably not a great idea. Do you want to go get some dessert somewhere?"

"I have an idea," I suggested as we climbed into his vehicle. "Why don't we swing by and pick it up to go?"

"Where am I taking us?" he replied with a sexy grin.

"Well, you already took me to one of your favorite spots. So let's go to one of mine." He started up the truck and pulled out of the lot.

The expression on his face looked innocent, yet like trouble all at the same time. For a girl denying any romantic intentions earlier… I had a feeling that was all about to change.

CHAPTER 6

We stopped by a bakery called Sweet Cheeks and picked up some carrot cake, a piece of chocolate pie, and some type of peanut butter parfait. It was definitely overboard, but we had a hard time narrowing down all of our choices. As we drove away, I gave him directions that led back to my apartment.

"Ah, I get it. You con me into getting you enough dessert to last you a week and then you want to be dropped off at your own house to eat it all by yourself. I've been duped," he said playfully.

"I want to show you something," I said, giving him mischievous eyes this time. We unloaded from the truck and he carried our bag of desserts inside. I quickly checked on all of the animals, adding some water to the tortoise's area and giving Dexter a good belly scratch followed by a bowl of food. He already ate before I headed out, but it just seemed cruel to head upstairs with a huge bag of desserts while he was left alone again.

Cole followed my lead up to the second story, then up another small, narrow stairway to the roof of the condo. The door opened to a furnished rooftop area complete with a sofa, a couple lounge chairs, two side tables, and a small fire pit table in the center. The couch faced towards the lake. At night the actual water was hard to see unless the moon was shining right on it, but the stars looked magnificent from here and the lights from downtown twinkled in the distance. It was my absolute favorite spot to sit and unwind.

"This is your view?" he said in amazement, looking around each direction. "It's incredible up here. You have a view of the lake? This is unreal."

"I feel like I spend more time up here than I do inside," I admitted, setting the desserts on one of the small tables. I turned the fire pit key and a soft orange glow illuminated from the table in front of the sofa.

Cole sat down next to me on the couch. His leg rested against mine, and I had no desire to protest his proximity. At least half the couch was still open, but I didn't mind.

We dug our plastic forks into the desserts, sampling each one and commenting how amazing they were.

"I think I would eat all of my meals up here," he stated, leaning back into the couch cushions. "I just can't get over how beautiful this spot is."

"Can you see the lake from your place?" I asked. "Where exactly do you live?"

"I'm much further west," he answered, resting his arm on the back of the couch. I knew if I leaned back I would essentially be leaning right up against him. I wasn't sure I could handle that. I was sincere about my lack of intent on dating anyone seriously. It just wasn't the right time for me. But sitting this close to Cole was quickly clouding my judgment. "No lake view from my place. I don't have a good view of anything, really. But I can get to the beach within a ten minute walk, so it works for me."

"Why would you want to leave all of this for southern California?" I questioned, referencing his comment about that earlier. I wasn't sure how serious he was about it.

"For a change," he shrugged. "I just want to pack a bag, get on my bike, and ride down the coast. I want to buy some land somewhere, hopefully some place I can see the ocean. I want to surf every morning. And I want to build my own house. Something simple. And I want fruit trees everywhere, and definitely avocado trees. I want to be able to make fresh guacamole any time I want. That's the life."

"That sounds like a good plan," I agreed, slowly leaning back in case he wanted the chance to move his arm out of the way. Instead it came down around my side. I shifted a bit sideways so I was facing him a little better. I wanted to look at him while we talked. "So what, you'll build a house, surf all day, and eat avocados? That's it?"

"Of course not, I'll own a bike shop too," he said confidently. "I've gotta make some money so my wife doesn't have to work if she doesn't want to."

"Oh yeah? And this wife, are you also picking her up riding down the coast?" I said with a playful laugh.

"Maybe," he replied with a boyish smirk. "Maybe I'll kidnap one until she grows to love me. Other than being charged with a felony, what could go wrong?" We both laughed. "What about you? If you could do anything, what would it be?"

"Honestly, I want to open up an animal rescue sanctuary," I said dreamily. "I want land and a few barns, and fences…"

"And avocado trees?" he suggested.

"I guess that wouldn't be so bad. I probably would need a garden to keep up with feeding all of the animals. So yeah, I need lots of land and space."

"You seem to be doing a good job already in your two-bedroom condo," he said genuinely.

"It's so frustrating, all of these animals that people just give up on," I explained. "Dr. Nikki, the vet at the clinic, she's my hero. She takes in every single one she gets a call on, even when she's over capacity at the clinic. She has a bunch of them at her house too, and then the overflow from that comes to me. She runs a great website to get them all re-homed. It's really inspiring. I would give anything to be able to help as many animals as she does."

"So that's why you went into veterinary science? To run a rescue? That's what you've always wanted to do?"

"Not exactly," I continued. "My parents were pushing for pre-med. My dad is a cardiologist, and he seemed to mistake my listening to his endless medical stories as interest to also become a doctor. I didn't know what I wanted to do, but it wasn't that. I just wanted out of the city though. Chicago is amazing in its own way, but I just wanted something *different.* Dr. Nikki is an old friend of my mom's from college. After my mom passed, I came out here one summer to visit her, just to clear my head and get away from all the noise of the city. I absolutely loved the area as soon as I saw it. It was so different from everything back home, and I knew I needed that kind of change. She convinced me to come out here for school and as soon as I saw her working in the clinic, I was hooked. That's when I realized what direction I wanted to head."

"So the Washington thing you mentioned last night, what's that? You're not continuing with school?" he asked, sounding genuinely interested.

"That was someone else's dream, not mine," I replied quietly. "I was going there for someone else."

"So now you're doing what you want instead?" he asked sweetly.

"I'm trying," I admitted. "But it's hard. You know, trying to figure it all out."

"Well for now this seems pretty good," he said, lightening the mood. "Dessert, stars, a handsome stranger."

"I could do worse," I admitted.

He shifted his body against the arm of the sofa with his legs at an angle. He motioned for me to slide sideways so that I was up against his torso, both of us looking up at the sky.

"Do you know any of the constellations?" he asked, mesmerized by the scene overhead.

"Just a few basics, nothing fancy. We didn't have stars like this in the city. I feel deprived now that I know just how beautiful they are in a place like this. I can't believe I spent all of those years looking at this same sky and I never realized all that was up there."

He pointed to a few, explaining some of them to me. He knew stories about the constellations I had never heard of in school. He named some that sounded so unfamiliar to me I wondered if he was making them up.

"How do you know so much about the constellations?" I questioned. "I wouldn't have pegged you for a science nerd."

"That's all Harvey, he taught me all about them when I was a kid," he said with a shy tone as if he was slightly embarrassed. "I wasn't the easiest kid. I went through a lot with my mom and dad at a pretty young age, and sitting outside was the only way I would listen to Harvey at first. When it was dark out I felt invisible, but he always knew I was there, hanging around the cabins. He would start talking as if he was telling an audience, but I was the only one who could hear him."

"What happened to your parents?" I asked nervously, unsure if he felt comfortable enough to share it with me.

"My mom's been out of the picture for awhile," he said hesitantly. "I don't really remember her well. I think I was around four or five when she stopped coming by. She had a lot of addictions, and love wasn't one of them. She wasn't cruel to me or anything, don't get me wrong. She wasn't a bad mom. She just wasn't one at all. She was never sober long enough to know what to do. So she never really had a chance I guess."

He spoke so innocently, and I was so intrigued by his perspective. She sounded like a whole lot more than a bad mom, but he didn't sound like he harbored negative feelings about it. I couldn't understand how that was possible.

"My dad, that's another story. He was cruel on purpose. Not just to me, but to everyone. He had some ties to Harvey somehow, even though to this day I don't really know the details. We lived down the road from Harvey's property, and I think my dad did some work for him. Of course he was in and out of jail a lot though, so it wasn't really steady employment."

I shifted down until I was essentially laying across his lap so I could look at him as we spoke. It seemed like too personal of a story to be staring out in space as he explained his upbringing. I could see the emotion in his eyes as we talked, and it completely humanized him to me. Before now, he was this huge macho guy that seemed cool and unaffected. But this conversation was so different.

"I should stop talking, right?" he said, shaking his head. "I know all of this is not a selling point on who I am. It's a total cliché, guy on the wrong side of the tracks with a rough family. It's all stupid, really."

"It's not stupid, that was your life. That's what made you who you are. I think it matters."

"Nah, none of that made me who I am. Harvey. That's the guy who raised me. That's who I am."

"So he took you in when your dad went off to jail?" I clarified, trying to understand the entire timeline. I couldn't say I ever knew anyone personally with this crazy of a back story. It was fascinating.

"Yeah, pretty much. I was at school one day, waiting to be picked up. I waited for so long the sun started going down, but no one ever came for me. It took me almost an hour to walk home that night, and no one was there when I showed up. Eventually Harvey realized the situation. He found me lurking around his property when I was supposed to be in class. He let me stay in one of his cabins and he forced me to go to school. I hated him for it for awhile, before I knew better.

He had rules and advice for me I didn't want. It took me awhile to realize that's what parents were for. I thought he was just a pain in my ass, quite honestly. But I get it now." He smiled down at me, brushing some of the hair off my face.

"So now you work for him," I said softly.

"Yeah, when he needs me," he answered considerately. "I have a hard time saying no to him, after everything he's done for me. But he knows there will come a day where I'll leave and get out on my own. I really do appreciate everything he's done for me, but this can't be it for me."

I smiled back up at him and he continued to gently touch the hair by my face.

"That's all I have for you tonight," he said jovially, changing the subject. "That's my life story. That's all the good stuff."

"I imagine there's a whole lot more," I replied, judging by the look on his face.

"Not tonight," he said back with a soft laugh. "You have to spend more time with me for that. I can't just give it all away for free. What about you? Tell me something personal about you."

"Sam's leaving in less than two months," I said with a sad tone in my voice. *So much for keeping the mood light.* The mere thought of her moving away made me all choked up. "I'm terrified of her leaving. I feel like I've never been alone before. I don't think I've ever been so scared of anything my whole life."

"Why does that scare you?" he asked directly. "If you've never been alone, how do you know it's so bad?"

I thoughtfully assessed his question. He actually had a good point.

"I've been alone most of my life," he continued, alternating his gaze from me up to the night sky. "Honestly being with someone seems far more terrifying," he said quietly.

"I actually agree with you on that," I muttered softly. "What about you? What scares you the most?"

"Honestly, after all I've been through in life, I don't think there's anything else to be scared of," he said with a macho tone. I guess he had something there. It sounded like he already lived through a nightmare when he was younger. Perhaps there really was nothing left to fear after something like that.

I gazed up at the night sky. It was amazing how I could look at the same view every single night, but it still awed me each time. I looked back at him and he was staring directly at me with a serious expression.

"What's that look for?" I questioned. The fire in front of us let off the perfect amount of heat for the slight chill in the air, but my skin still prickled as he reached out and softly grazed my arm with his fingertips.

"I'm just thinking," he said dismissively, shaking his head.

"I wish I could hear your thoughts," I replied honestly. He had more emotion in his eyes than he ever had in his words, and I always felt like there was more he wanted to say.

"I just wish I knew what he did to you," he said quietly, shaking his head again like he was frustrated.

"Who?"

"Whatever guy… The one who you think broke you." His gaze felt so protectively intense on me, but he looked angry at the same time. "Never mind, I know, it's not my business. But that look in your eyes when you're doubting yourself - when you want to pretend like you're not scared of something, or when you admit to me that you are – it's the same look. And I just wonder what happened. I can't help but want to hurt whoever did that to you."

My throat started to feel tight and I'm pretty sure my eyes began to moisten. I sat back up, facing him on the couch. "It's not a good story," I said reluctantly. Honestly I'd never told anyone before firsthand. My friends already knew about the entire thing when it happened, so I never had to actually rehash it to someone. It made me feel numb. I wasn't sure I could talk about it. "It's not what you think."

"I don't know what I think, honestly," he said, still keeping his eyes on mine. "I'm not making any judgments about it. I just want to know what happened."

"It's not the story all the other girls tell you," I said, feeling my throat further constrict. "I wasn't left or heartbroken or cheated on or something. Every girl I know from school, that's their thing, right? They trusted someone, he bailed, then every guy after that is an asshole. I know that's every girl's story."

"I've heard it, yeah," he said sympathetically.

"Well unfortunately for me, *I'm* the asshole in my own story," I admitted as a slow tear fell down my face. He gently wiped it away with his thumb.

"Despite this physique, I'm not a hero in all my stories either," he said with a sweet smile, making me laugh. Another tear fell at the same time.

"Are you sure you want to do this?" I asked nervously.

"Yes," he said confidently. "I've been the asshole too, I'm not proud of that. But whatever you're holding on to… Look, I'm no expert. But I imagine it's not so big that you have to carry around the burden from it forever."

"But it is," I said as another tear fell. They were getting harder to stop at this point, and I knew the flood was coming. "Ian, that was my ex," I tried explaining with a shaky voice. "He's…

well I…. He….” No matter how hard I tried to say it, the sentences wouldn't form.

Cole just stared back at me with empathetic eyes that were coaxing me to continue.

"We didn't want the same things," I began, trying to start further back. "I mean maybe I did at first, or maybe I *wanted* to want the same things…" I felt my brain shutting down again. "He was accepted into med school for neuroscience in Washington and had everything planned out for us, down to the high rise we would live in. I already lived that life in Chicago, and maybe I wasn't completely sure of what I wanted, but I knew it looked different than everything Ian was planning. I just, I hesitated… For a second, I hesitated. I panicked, and I thought maybe I could stop time and sort it all out. I merely said the words 'I'm not sure' and that was it. I was uncertain for one brief second, and that was it."

More tears fell down my face, and although I was certain Cole wasn't really following what I was rambling about, he reached out and pulled me into him. He softly stroked my hair.

"He got mad at me, rightfully so, I mean *I* was the one who hesitated. I wasn't sure I wanted to be part of the life he planned out with such complete precision. It just made me panic. I went out that night to some dumb party and I don't know, I just wanted to feel *nothing.* Because I felt really bad about the whole thing and I hated it, so I thought feeling nothing would somehow feel better. He called me that night and asked me if I really thought we shouldn't be together. Instead of talking about it, or coming up with a plan, or having some rational time to actually think about it, I just hung up the phone like we were disconnected. Because that's how I felt, completely *disconnected* from him. I drank some more, and then he called me around two in the morning. He wanted to have a serious conversation about it. I guess with the alcohol surging through me, I finally felt brave enough to talk about it. But I couldn't drive, I knew that. So I told him to come and get me."

The tears poured out of my eyes now, and I knew there was no way to hold them back. Cole continued to hold me, not saying anything, but instead just letting me speak as I felt ready.

"On his way to come pick me up, he was in a bad accident," I said quietly. My voice cut out and I wondered how I would get the words out. "He was hit on the driver's side by a semi. We never got to finish our conversation. I never had the opportunity to make up for the cruelty I left him with. He died instantly. That's how he left the world – with my hesitation and uncertainty. He didn't deserve that."

My tears were unrelenting sobs by this point. My throat hurt so bad and my eyes burned, and I felt outside of my own body. I had cried so many tears after the incident happened, I thought it would be impossible to have any more left. But here I was, feeling as broken as I did in the early morning hours when I got the call. I felt like an empty shell of a person. I sat there that night for an hour, waiting on the steps of some unfamiliar house, waiting to be picked up by someone who did nothing wrong other than promising to love me forever. But he never came to get me. I felt my own sense of abandonment in that moment, just sitting there, waiting. Then the cold news came from a phone call I received from a stranger. Nothing prepares you for a moment like that – the second before you realize your entire world is about to change. It felt then like I was falling from the top of a building – and somehow it still felt like I was falling now. I wasn't sure if hitting the ground at any point would be my penance or my rebirth, free from the guilt I held onto. I hated that no matter how much time had passed, the whole thing hit me in the chest and knocked the wind out of me. It numbed my whole body.

I closed my eyes, as it felt like my only solution to hold on to the slightest possibility that the entire thing, my hesitation, Ian's reaction to fix it, all of it – perhaps there was still a chance it could all be a dream.

The saddest part – I wasn't sure at what part of that story I wanted to wake up to.

CHAPTER 7

My phone rang, startling me out of a deep sleep. I felt disoriented and confused. My bedroom clock read seven, but I wasn't sure if that meant morning or night. *Why was I wearing my clothes and not pajamas?* I didn't even remember getting in bed.

I answered my phone with a scratchy voice.

"Hello?"

"I just wanted to make sure you were up in time for work," Cole's smooth voice said on the other end. "You were pretty out of it last night."

I thought back to the events of our rooftop soiree. Did I fall asleep on him last night?

"How did I get in my bed?" I asked, still confused by exactly what happened.

"I carried you there. It was starting to get cool out. I wasn't going to let you sleep outside by yourself," he said sweetly.

"Why didn't you stay?"

"Because you didn't ask me to," he replied softly.

"Why am I still in my clothes?" I added, looking down at my jeans and wrinkled white blouse.

"Because I prefer my women conscious before I undress them," he teased. "You didn't even stir when I carried you downstairs."

"Well thank you," I said, grateful he couldn't see me blushing. "You're still calling me after our conversation last night?"

"Of course, why wouldn't I? Do you really think that changed anything for me?"

"I don't know," I replied honestly. Surely there was some kind of guy code where if a girl sobbed on the first date, he was supposed to run for the hills. But yet here he was, seeming completely un-phased by knowing the worst thing I'd ever done.

"Nothing's changed, Syd," he answered quickly. "Seven fifteen tonight?"

"Yeah," I responded. I had to admit, now that I was thinking about spending more time with him tonight, I was a little bummed that our meet-up would be so short, but I was looking forward to it nonetheless. "Thanks for the wake-up call. Next time you can stay, you know. I don't want you driving home in the middle of the night." *Yeah, as if a guy like Cole was remotely unsafe out in the dark on his own.*

"For a girl off the market, you're not making this easy on me." I could hear the smile in his voice.

"Sorry, you're right. I'm giving you mixed messages," I admitted, not sure what exactly was happening between us. I was obviously a mess. "I just like your company, that's all." *And the way your lips feel. And the way your body felt pressed up against mine on the couch.* I shook away those thoughts.

"Well at this rate, you'll get plenty of me," he said with a cheerful voice. "You're still up for going to the bonfire with me tomorrow night?"

"Of course," I replied, thankful he couldn't see how big my grin was at the moment.

"Perfect. Then I'll see you tonight at seven fifteen."

We hung up and I was beaming. I genuinely enjoyed being around him, I knew that much. Last night under the stars felt like perfection – dessert, real conversation, my body leaned up against him… I wished I hadn't fallen apart on him, that was the ultimate disappointment, but yet that entire admission needed to happen. Not to mention my brain at the moment didn't want to even think about what would've happened if I kept my mouth shut and actually stayed awake. I definitely wasn't ready for that yet.

I forced myself out of bed and into the shower, taking the extra time to dry my hair since today was my late start. I introduced Dexter to the tortoise, and he was surprisingly gentle with him. I rummaged through my closet, trying to decide what to wear tonight. I would only have a few minutes to change after work before he arrived, so I wanted to plan for it now.

We were probably only going to see each other for a brief amount of time. He had somewhere to be, so I imagined if we were even lucky enough to see the turtles hatch, our time together wouldn't stretch too far beyond that.

Today's forecast was a little warmer than it had been the past few days, so I opted for a casual skirt that hit just above my knees and a tank top with a fitted sweater over it. It still looked somewhat casual, but definitely turned it up a notch from the jeans yesterday. *Was that even what I was trying to do? Turn it 'up' a notch? What exactly did that even mean?* Honestly I hadn't even really sorted out my intentions with Cole. I liked being around him though, which was good enough for now.

Before heading to the clinic, I made sure to text Sam so she wouldn't be waiting all day to hear from me. '*Wish I had more for you, but after crying in front of him, I fell asleep during the middle of my date last night.*' I added the scream face emoji after that. I figured she was probably already in class by now, so I likely wouldn't even get a response from her until around lunchtime, or possibly later.

I made it into the clinic a few minutes before my shift and everyone already working turned to stare at me. I was thankful the only customer at the moment was leaving.

"Story time," Eva said, clasping her excited hands together. "Tell us everything."

"There's not a lot to tell," I replied, trying to keep it somewhat vague. "We had tacos and then went back to my place, where I proceeded to fall asleep in the middle of our conversation. He let himself out. Those are the highlights." I left out the crying part for obvious reasons.

"Oh Syd," Dr. Nikki chimed in, "I'm running you ragged here. You've been picking up extra shifts and you were too exhausted to even enjoy it." I could hear the sympathy in her voice.

"No, I'm fine," I stated, brushing off her worry. "It was just a long day. I appreciate the extra shifts, you know I'm trying to save up for the fall." *Although the truth was, I didn't have plans to head back for more schooling, so honestly I didn't even know why I was working so hard to save up for anything. I still had no plan.*

"Are you going to see him again? Give me more!" Eva said dramatically. "My love life is dead, I have to live through you."

"Well that's going to be a disappointment," I replied with a giggle. "But Sam, wait until you see her tomorrow. She finally met someone. She's going out with him on Saturday." I left the details out that I would be seeing more of Cole, but it seemed helpful to point the attention towards Sam. At least it would get them off my back.

"At least one of you girls is living the life," Eva said before answering an incoming call.

I made my way to the back and put away my stuff. I knew we had a pretty full workload today.

Sure enough we had seven surgeries and a few other minor procedures. Sam stopped in briefly around lunchtime on her break from class. I quickly explained the night before, keeping it unimpressive. I didn't want her getting her hopes up that there was anything more going on. After all, maybe he was just being polite by calling this morning. My actions had to at least make him a little wary.

The rest of the afternoon passed quickly which I was thankful for. Around five, my phone finally chimed with a text from Cole's number. *'Assuming you don't have time for dinner before we meet up, I've got it covered.'* I replied back with a simple message. *'Sounds good.'*

"We're not going to need any more help tonight," Dr. Nikki said around six p.m. as I cleaned up from our last scheduled procedure. "You can head back home. Catch up on your sleep, or some other plans?" she said, hinting she knew I had somewhere to be tonight. "I'll keep you on the clock til seven anyway, but if you stick around you'll just be bored. So get out of here, do something restful or fun." She smiled at me warmly.

"Thank you," I replied sincerely. She was always good to me like that.

I grabbed my stuff and made the short walk back home. I was so relieved to have the extra time. I rinsed my body, hoping to get rid of the animal smell I was around all day. That was definitely one of the downsides to working in a vet clinic. I threw a few curls in my hair and I reapplied my makeup, feeling refreshed. Right at seven-fifteen, there was a knock at my door. A huge smile spread across my face, but then I forced myself to hold it back a little as I opened the door so I wouldn't seem too eager. Unfortunately as soon as I saw him, I couldn't keep it in.

"And I thought you looked beautiful when you were passed out drooling last night," he teased with a low whistle. "Geez."

"Nice to see you too," I stated, locking the door behind me. I was thankful to see he had his truck again.

He helped me climb into the cab and we headed towards the beach across from Antonio's.

"Are you hungry?" he asked politely.

"Starving," I replied. "It was a long day at the clinic. Are we having tacos again?" I smiled at him from the passenger seat.

"Something less fancy," he said with a wink.

"Did you work today?" I was curious as to what his day-to-day really looked like since he didn't seem to have a conventional job or schedule.

"A little." He didn't offer any more than that.

"So secretive," I said coyly. I wasn't sure why he wasn't more forthcoming with this stuff by now, especially after learning something so personal about me. We had plans together four nights in a row, so clearly it made sense that I'd be interested to know more about him.

"Why do you want to know so much?" he asked me with a raised brow. "Maybe the not knowing is part of my charm." He flashed me a handsome, genuine smile and it melted me. "Besides, I told you all of my secrets only come out after midnight, remember?"

"Then it's unfortunate I'm not more of a night owl," I replied flirtatiously as he pulled into the parking lot of Antonio's where we'd parked the night before. We climbed out of the truck and he grabbed a giant bag, swinging it over his shoulder. He gently slid his other hand in mine as if that's where it belonged; as if he'd done it hundreds of times before. I wondered if he did it out of some kind of habit – maybe he was doing this kind of thing far more often than I imagined. Or maybe he did it as more of a chivalrous, protective gesture since we were crossing a somewhat busy street. Either way, I was more than happy to be attached to him.

We made our way to the spot on the beach over by the rocks. He set the bag down and checked on the turtle eggs.

"I think we're in luck tonight," he said excitedly. I peered over to where he was pointing and there was some slight movement in the sand as the eggs subtly shifted. "We probably have a little bit of time though. They usually wait until the sun is down so it's harder for predators to find them."

"So you studied biology or zoology or something in school?" I pried, staring at his handsome face. It seemed somewhat strange to me that a guy like this would know so much about turtles.

"No, like I said, Harvey taught me pretty much everything I know," he answered with a hint of nostalgia in his voice. "Let's eat."

He pulled a sheet out of his bag and spread it across the sand. We sat down on it together, closely in the middle, and he pulled some food out as well.

"You made sandwiches?" I asked with an amused tone. They appeared to be homemade, which seemed sweet and unexpected.

"We could be here longer than I think," he replied with a shrug. "You never really know how long something like this could take. I have fruit, chips, brownies… I didn't make those though," he continued, rummaging through the bag. He handed me a Sprite, no doubt picking up on that as my drink of choice the night before.

"So do you cook?" I asked curiously.

"Yes, sandwiches," he answered with a laugh. "And Mexican food. It's not as good as Antonio's, but I'm trying. My enchiladas are amazing. But other than that, if the food doesn't go on bread or in a tortilla, I'm useless."

"Hence your desire for avocado trees," I stated, bringing up our conversation from the night before. That's when our banter was good – before the crying and the part where I passed out. "I'm sorry for falling asleep on you last night," I added bashfully. "That was pretty embarrassing. Of course I'm not sure if that part was better or worse than the sobbing. Probably the best first date you've ever had, huh?"

"So you're finally admitting that was actually a date?" he said with piqued interest.

"Any night that ends with me crying and then sleeping alone, yeah… That's pretty much my dating life to a tee," I answered sarcastically. "I'm surprised you even showed up to get me tonight."

The sun finally sank all the way behind the mountain tops and the water looked calm under the moon's glow. It seemed crazy to me that just a few nights ago we'd met after the incident out front of the clinic, and now here we were having a picnic on the beach after a simple sunset. Something this random was surely fleeting. It made no sense. There was obviously a reason he had so many secrets. I wondered if I would learn even one of them.

"I meant what I said this morning," he said softly, staring at my face. "Everything you said last night, I understand it's a big thing for you. But it doesn't change anything. You really thought I wouldn't show up after that?"

"I don't know," I answered quietly. I understood what he was saying – maybe it wasn't something big to *him*. But I felt like it was a huge turning point for me, to finally be able to share that with someone else. I hadn't uttered a word about the entire situation since shortly after the incident happened. I had to admit, it felt good to get out, but I also felt crazy for saying it out loud. It felt better as a secret. Now that it was out in the open, I felt like just another crazy girl with some sort of complication.

"You're looking at me differently," he said with a shy smirk.

"I am?" I blushed. I wasn't sure what he meant by it.

"You are. But I'm not looking at you any differently. I just want you to know that."

Butterflies swirled all around my insides and I immediately took a bite of my sandwich to hide my grin. I didn't want his words to rattle me in such an obvious way.

"We should check the turtles again," I chimed in, changing the subject.

"Yeah, the turtles," he repeated with a smile, likely figuring out exactly what I was doing. Serious conversations often made me panic. I think he was picking up on that. "The ever-important turtles." He winked at me and then turned to walk over to the rocks.

I smiled as I watched him, noticing his muscles tighten as he bent forward. *Oh what I would give to –*

"Syd, get up!" he said urgently. "Come here!"

I leapt up from the sheet, quickly setting the rest of my sandwich down. I hurried over to where he was standing, and sure enough, there was movement. The tiniest turtles I'd ever laid eyes on climbed out of their shells and quickly made their way to the water. I squealed as they hurried past us, completely in awe of what I was watching. Nature amazed me, the way these tiny creatures knew exactly what to do at the right moment. Then you had advanced humans like me, who couldn't figure out which direction to go at any given moment.

"They're so cute!" I exclaimed, watching them slide through the sand.

"Oh no, this is how it starts, right? You want to take them all home with you, don't you?" he chuckled.

"Only if there's an abandoned one left over," I joked back. He leaned over, wrapping a strong arm around my waist. His eyes burned through me and I wanted so much more from him than a beach picnic.

"So then you'll keep me?" he said quietly. I'm sure he meant it to be playful or sarcastic, but there seemed to be more to it in his voice. He *was* abandoned. I was so thankful for Harvey in that moment, a man I didn't even know. For him to look at an abandoned boy and decide he was worth keeping – that was something really beautiful.

"You don't have to decide now, but think about it," he teased, breaking up my thoughts. He slowly leaned in and his lips met mine. They were warm and sweet and inviting. Any light left over from the setting sun was completely gone now, and the night sky enveloped us. He pulled me in even closer and kissed me hungrily. Whatever I was running from before this moment, it seemed so distant now.

"I'm willing to give it strong consideration," I said breathily as he slowly pulled away from me. He stared into my eyes, probably trying to read my thoughts.

"I'm not trying to pressure you into anything," he said sweetly. "As long as you agree to keep hanging out with me, I can live with that." He flashed me such a sexy grin that I couldn't imagine a moment I *didn't* want to spend with him.

"It's such a shame you have a poker game to get to," I said suggestively. I hated that he had somewhere to be. I wasn't ready for the night to end any time soon.

"Who says I have to go?" he replied with a smirk and a raised brow. "I've cancelled for far less." He leaned in again and kissed me, slowly at first, then with more intensity. Something about that moment, with our bodies pressed together and our feet in the sand, it felt like the epitome of summer.

Cole's phone rang loudly, but he didn't loosen his arm around me. I felt his lips curl up into a smile as he tried swatting his pants to get the sound to stop.

"I'm so sorry," he whispered in between kisses, "I can't get it to shut off." The sound finally stopped and he brought his hands up to my face, kissing me again. Seconds later, the ringing phone sounded again. "I'm gonna throw it in the lake," he teased, pulling away from me this time to get it out of his jeans.

"Sounds like someone is trying to find you," I replied, watching him fumble for his phone. His face had such a jovial expression – until he saw the screen.

"Shit," he muttered, looking immediately frustrated. "I have to get you home."

"Is it my father?" I teased, still trying to keep the mood light.

"Hello?" he answered sternly, completely changing his tone from seconds earlier. "Yeah. Okay. I can be there in less than ten minutes." He paused. "I know, but I have to make a stop, less than ten."

He hung up the phone, looking irritated. "I have to take you home," he repeated abruptly, turning towards our picnic spot. In one swift motion he gathered up the sheet in his arms, shoving the entire thing, food and all, back into the bag.

"Where do you have to go? I could come with you?" I offered, studying his face. Realistically speaking, it would definitely save him some time if he was in a hurry so he wouldn't have to take me back home. Not to mention I wasn't ready to leave him for the night.

"I can't," he said quietly, grabbing my hand to lead me back across the street to his truck. "I'm sorry, I just can't."

He didn't elaborate, and his response felt cold. We walked back to the truck and he didn't even open my door. He just threw the bag in the back of the truck and quickly climbed in. I did as well.

We drove back to my condo in silence, which strangely echoed loudly in my head somehow. I wanted to know so badly why he was shutting me out, but I felt too uncomfortable to ask in that moment. He clearly wasn't talking for a reason.

We pulled up to my door and he didn't shut off the engine.

"Will I still see you tomorrow night for the bonfire, or…" I said hesitantly, not finishing my sentence.

"Yes," he replied, finally breaking his serious expression with a half smile. "I'm sorry for all of this."

"Do you want to tell me what's going on?" I didn't want to push him, but I wanted to let him know that I genuinely cared.

"It's probably better if you don't know," he said quietly, leaning over and kissing my cheek. "I'll call you tomorrow?"

"Sure," I shrugged, unsure how to break him down to get him to open up to me. "If you want."

"Syd, this had nothing to do with you. This doesn't change our plans or anything," he said a little defensively. "You don't want to know about the kind of stuff I deal with."

"You're wrong," I replied softly. "I do. If you think my secrets aren't so bad that they'll change your opinion of me, why do you think it's different for you?"

He finally made eye contact with me, staring at me with a deep, soulful expression.

"Because my secrets are worse," he whispered.

CHAPTER 8

I had a restless night of sleep. There were moments where I stared at the ceiling trying to eradicate Cole completely from my brain. I barely knew him, nothing personal or intimate anyway – that was his doing – so it would sure be a hell of a lot easier to walk away from him now.

But then I had moments where I would stare at my phone as the minutes passed, hoping he would call and win me back over with his soothing, charming voice. I felt so comfortable around him, in a very short amount of time – that never happened to me. It was easy for me to stay guarded and uninterested when other guys approached me, but with Cole, it was obvious he was breaking my guard down easily. *Probably because of those arms.* Thoughts like those weren't helping me sleep either.

I was already stirring when my alarm went off at five. At least I would have Sam with me at the clinic today – that was enough to get me out of bed.

Sure enough we both arrived at the clinic a few minutes before six. I felt like we had so much to catch up on, though barely any time had passed. I wanted to call her last night, but I hoped to hear from Cole first so I would be less agitated by the whole thing, but that never happened.

As we put our stuff away in the break room, I filled Sam in on the last two nights. She seemed excited when I told her about our kiss on the beach after the turtles, but she agreed with me that everything after that was a disappointment.

"So what do you think it was? Why do you think he left? You must at least have some assumptions," Sam mused.

"It could be anything," I shrugged. "I don't even know what the guy does for a living."

"Do you think it's something as bad as he led on?" she asked skeptically.

"Probably," I admitted. "I think he definitely has something shady going on." I hated the reality of that, but it had to be true. He was honest with me about his upbringing – that was personal. But everything else he ever said was cryptic. I wondered if he was right – maybe it was better if I didn't know too much.

Our workday was a lot more fun and laid back than I expected it to be. Dr. Nikki always kept the surgeries light on Friday, which we all appreciated. The bad news, however, came towards the end of my shift.

"Dexter officially has a forever home," Dr. Nikki said excitedly. "They can't make it in today before closing though, so they'll be in Monday to pick him up. Your house will finally get a whole lot quieter."

"I haven't minded it at all," I stated honestly. I was actually going to miss his company, he was so much fun to play with. The squeals he let out before mealtimes or when he wanted attention didn't really phase me. I strangely liked the sound.

"Well give him a lot of love over the weekend," she continued, "and you can just bring him in with you Monday morning. I'll do one last checkup before he heads out."

I felt a small knot in my stomach. It happened every time I had to give one of the animals up. I knew from the beginning that my time with them was just temporary, but it still affected me every time they left. I was always saddened by the thought of never seeing them again, but also nervous they *would* return if someone else gave up on them. That was the ultimate heartbreak for me.

My phone rang, distracting me from the news about Dexter.

"Three minutes," I said quickly towards Sam so she would cover for me while I headed out the back door for some privacy. My stomach flipped when I saw Cole's name on the screen.

"Hello?" I answered casually.

"Am I bothering you at work or are you off yet?" he asked politely.

"I'm done in about a half hour," I explained, not saying any more. I wanted him to lead the conversation. I wasn't sure what I even wanted from him anymore.

"Do you want me to call you back?"

"No, I can talk. It's pretty slow this afternoon," I confessed.

"First of all, I obviously owe you an apology. I am so sorry about last night," he explained in a sincere voice. "Harvey got some pretty serious threats last night, and we had a lot of stuff to move from the warehouse. I'd never heard him panic like that, so I knew it was serious. I was a little rattled and I didn't handle that well at all. I've been thinking about it all day long."

"I think this is where I pretend that I haven't given it any thought at all," I replied, feeling it impossible to be mad at him for it after his heartfelt words.

"Look, it was a douche move. I know that," he sighed. "I know I need to tell you more about it... About me... Everything." He fell quiet. "I already lied to you once."

Maybe this wasn't starting off as well as I thought.

"Do you remember the other night when you asked me if I was scared of anything?" he questioned with some hesitation in his voice.

"Yes," I replied softly. "And in your best macho voice you said nothing. You have no fears whatsoever."

"I knew that was a lie as soon as I said it," he admitted. "After meeting you, I feel like now I'm scared of everything."

"What do you mean?" I asked with genuine curiosity.

"I don't know, it's everything," he reiterated, as if I knew what that meant. "I know I'll lose you if I'm *not* honest with you. You deserve that from me. But I know I'll lose you if I *am*." There was a pause. "I mean I know you're not even mine to lose," he said, trying to clarify his thoughts. "Look, can we talk about this in person? I need to see you looking at me when I talk so I can gauge how stupid I sound." I smiled, feeling relieved by whatever he was or wasn't saying. He was at least trying.

"What time are you picking me up?" I asked, trying to hide how anxious I was to see him.

"The party doesn't even start until nine, and I have to wrap up some stuff before then. So like eight forty-five?"

It was later than I'd hoped, but I was thrilled about our plans nonetheless.

"I'll see you then," I said casually. We hung up the phone and I instantly felt like I was going to burst with nervous excitement. Cole's words gave me the impression that maybe he was finally ready to open up to me a little more. I was so anxious for that to happen. I headed back into the clinic and Sam could immediately tell by my expression that I was delirious.

"So all is well?" she asked, cleaning up one of the exam rooms. I helped get all of the linens to the wash pile and we sanitized all of the equipment.

"He's picking me up a little before nine," I shrugged. A huge smile spread across my face.

"What's happening tomorrow then? Are we still heading out on a boat with Luke?" she asked, her excitement matching mine.

"Yeah, that hasn't changed," I stated. "I think we're still planning to meet up around two. I'll text you in the morning. In the meantime, do you want to catch some sun this afternoon?"

"Yes," she happily agreed as we finished up our shift. Like so many other afternoons, we headed back to my condo to change and then made our way down to the beach. It was another perfect summer day without a cloud in the sky. We joined in a volleyball game that was already going on and the beach seemed busier than usual, probably because it was a Friday afternoon versus a regular weekday. We grabbed some grub from a nearby burger joint and finally separated around six.

I took a full shower and took my time drying and curling my hair. Tonight felt big. I imagined I would be meeting some of his friends – maybe that alone would give me some more insight as to what Cole was all about. He'd already met Sam and Brandt, so I was excited to meet some of his friends as well. I hoped we would have some time to break away and talk too – I felt like we needed that at this point.

I wasn't exactly sure what to wear for the night. In college we'd had some late night beach parties, sure, but we were usually in our college sweatshirts, which didn't seem appropriate for tonight. I chose another skirt like the one I wore last night, cotton and casual, with a fitted shirt and a light sweatshirt for the cool night air. I threw on some old sandals and was ready in plenty of time before Cole arrived.

He picked me up in his truck again, which I was so thankful for. I wondered if I would ever feel comfortable enough to ride on his motorcycle. I was surprised he hadn't asked me about it yet.

As we walked to his truck he gently squeezed my hand and I swear I felt it through my entire body. He helped me into his vehicle and stopped before turning away, leaning in to kiss me. "No early night tonight," he said quietly, studying my face. "Are you ready to see how the other half live?"

"What does that mean?" I said with a slight laugh.

"I imagine you've never been to a West Cove bonfire, right?" he said with a smirk as he climbed into the truck and started the engine. "Don't expect anything fancy."

"It's a beach with a fire pit and probably excessive alcohol, how different can it be from any other party? Maybe I'm not as sheltered as you think," I said mockingly.

"We'll see about that," he teased back. "Do you want to discuss safe words in case things get weird?"

"Seriously?" I asked with a scrunched up face and a light laugh. "Where are you really taking me?"

"Just blink twice if you want me to throw you over my shoulder and carry you out of there," he continued. We drove west towards the dive bar we were in the other night, but then continued even beyond that. As we headed down one of the side streets, a woman caught my eye.

"Slow down, I think I know her," I said, pointing to the woman up ahead.

"I can't imagine you know anyone around here," he muttered, slowing his truck down a bit.

"I do, Sam and I used to give her sandwiches after our shift at the clinic on the weekends," I said, recognizing her from her worn yellow shoes. "She looks like she needs help."

"You know Crazy Jamie?" he replied in disbelief. "I hope you're kidding."

"Maybe she needs a ride or something, she looks lost."

"For the record, you would never actually pick up a hitchhiker, right?" he asked, looking over at me.

"Stop the truck," I directed as we caught up to her.

"What do you want to do?" he asked skeptically, pulling the truck over. The woman in the yellow shoes didn't even seem to notice a vehicle had stopped behind her. She just kept slowly walking.

"I don't know, maybe she needs money or she's hungry or something. She told me she has kids. Why would she be out this late?"

"Syd, there are a lot of reasons people are out this late around here, but none of those reasons are usually good ones," he said protectively. "I see her around here all the time. She's bat shit crazy. I've never seen her with kids."

"Just give me a minute," I said, reaching for the door handle.

"Whoa, no," he said, reaching over me. "Syd, I think this is a bad idea, I don't want you getting out of the truck."

I studied his face as he said it. His tone was somewhat domineering, but I believed he had good intentions. "I haven't seen her in a couple months, she looks so frail. I want to help her," I said sincerely. I rummaged through my purse. "I have some money we can…"

"Stay here," he answered reluctantly, cutting me off. He climbed out of the truck, pushing the door lock behind him.

I watched as he approached the woman, rolling down my window just slightly to catch the conversation.

"Cr, uh, Jamie," he said, catching himself on the nickname. "Your name is Jamie, right?"

"Aren't you one of them Harlow boys? I'm not looking for any trouble," she sneered.

"That's not why I'm here," he said softly. "My girl, she's in the truck, she knows you. She said she used to give you food outside of the Mountain Ridge Vet Clinic?"

"Ah, those girls," Jamie said with a fondness in her voice, "let me guess, that pretty blonde one? I never did know her name…"

"Yes, Sydney. She hasn't seen you in awhile and just wanted me to check on you. Are you okay, do you need anything?" Cole asked her sincerely. He looked up at me in the truck and I smiled back at him.

Her response was muffled, and I wasn't sure what she was saying to him. He reached into his wallet and handed her some bills. She patted him on the arm and he walked back to the truck. I quickly hit the unlock button so he could climb back in.

"What did I just do," he groaned with a laugh.

"You helped someone, what do you mean?"

"I think I just gave her drug money," he said, shaking his head at me. "Do you really do that kind of thing?"

"I try to," I said honestly. "I mean not drug money, they should use it for food. There aren't exactly a lot of homeless people in Mountain Ridge, I don't know where they all go, but if I saw someone who needed something, yes, I would help them. You have to try."

"You're going to get eaten alive on the west side," he muttered, still shaking his head. "You're really something."

"What's that supposed to mean?" I said playfully.

"Nothing bad," he replied, flashing me a huge grin. "Just please, don't come over to this side of town. You don't need to see just how many people really need something. You won't make it out of here. Or worse, you'll start collecting humans instead of animals," he teased.

"Is it that bad over here?" I inquired. Honestly I hadn't ventured out much, but I couldn't imagine anywhere near Lake Tahoe was really *that* bad.

He was still shaking his head in disbelief over what had just happened as we headed further down the road. Finally we pulled into a wooded area that led us to a decent-sized parking lot. He parked the truck and I saw a few other people walking from their vehicles towards the beach.

"Just promise me you'll stay close," he said protectively. "No wandering off to help crazy people."

"Come on, she wasn't that bad," I replied, reaching for the door handle. Before I could pull it open, Cole slid over and pressed his lips on mine.

"Just stay close," he reiterated. "And remember, we don't have to stay here long. If it's not fun, we can go." We climbed out of the truck and headed towards the bonfire. It was actually a pretty impressive blaze and there were quite a few people there. Guys cheerfully greeted Cole, asking where he'd been recently like they hadn't seen him around for awhile. There were groups of girls standing around with red solo cups, looking me up and down. I wished they looked a little more friendly, but I understood I was the outsider here. Everyone else seemed to know each other.

"Hey man, glad you made it," a stocky dark haired guy said to Cole as they half-embraced.

"Yeah, it's been a bit," Cole interjected. "Sydney, this is Rick." He shook my hand and I politely said hello, still conscious of all of the eyes on me.

"Hey man, can you help me with one of the kegs real quick?" Rick asked Cole.

"Um, yeah," he replied reluctantly, looking at me. "Let me grab Luke and Tyler real quick, she knows them."

Cole led me towards the fire where I recognized the two guys from Soul Punch. I smiled to myself, still unable to stop the amusement I got from that stupid band name. I obviously didn't know them at all, but I guess they were the only familiar people around in the grand scheme of things. I suppose it would be nice to get to know the guy Sam was crushing on a little better.

"So, I'm still hanging with your girl Sam tomorrow, right?" Luke said as we approached them.

"Yeah man, two o'clock tomorrow?" Cole replied. "Hey, I'm gonna help Rick with the keg real quick, can Sydney stay here for a minute?" The two guys nodded. I was not looking forward to the awkward forced conversation.

"Great show the other night," I offered with a compulsory smile as Cole walked away. *So much for staying close to him all night. I wanted to blink twice so he would throw me over his shoulder and carry me away like he promised.*

"Yeah? Glad you liked it," Tyler replied, sipping on some drink out of a plastic cup. Luke was holding a beer bottle. "We're still working on some things, but it's really coming together. We're trying to fuse all of our influences together, so we're going for like a Beastie Boys meets Rage Against the Machine with a little early Metallica in there."

"Oh, that's the sound you're going for?" I stated, trying not to laugh. *That should not be a sound at all.* A few girls walked up to join our conversation.

"So, new girl tonight? Let me guess, you picked her up at a show?" a girl with dark hair said with a negative tone towards Luke and Tyler.

"Nah, this is Cole's girl," Tyler responded. I could see by her expression that she was displeased.

"Figures he would bring some Ridge City LC to the party," a tall blonde girl scoffed. I wasn't even sure what that meant. They walked away as quickly as they arrived, and I could hear them still talking about me as they left.

"Am I not welcome here?" I said, motioning my head towards the girls walking away.

"No, that's just Britt for you, the blonde one. She's Cole's ex," Luke said, shrugging them off. "She's always a bitch, even when she likes you. Don't pay attention to them."

Cole finally made his way back to us and I was so relieved.

"Sorry," he said sweetly to me, wrapping an arm around my shoulders. "None of these other jackwagons are strong enough to get the keg off the truck," he teased towards his friends. I imagined stuff like that happened to Cole often, the same way a tall co-worker of mine was always asked to get everything off the top shelf.

"Whatever man, we're musicians, we don't need muscles," Tyler responded playfully. "You guys want a drink?"

"Syd, do you want anything?" Cole asked courteously.

"No, thanks, I'm fine for now," I said politely.

"I don't need anything either right now man, but thanks," Cole replied.

"You guys are so lame," another guy stated walking up, joining in on the conversation. "Keg stands in ten, come join in." The guy walked away after he said it, joining another group of people behind us.

"So, are you impressed so far?" Cole teased as Luke and Tyler left us to go talk to some girls.

"It's a nice night out at least," I stated optimistically. "But the girls don't seem too friendly."

"Ignore them, come on," he said, grabbing my hand. "I want you to at least meet a few of my friends. Then if the party sucks we can go." He led me towards a couple guys standing on the other side of the fire. They were drinking beer and having an energetic conversation.

"Well look who showed up," a guy matching Cole's size exclaimed as we walked up to him.

"Sydney, this is my buddy Bryce. We work together at the bike shop," Cole introduced us. We shook hands politely.

"Well hot damn, I guess you didn't make her up," he teased Cole. "But Sydney, where are all your friends? Come on Cole, you can't bring a pretty girl to the party without her friends."

"Luke already has a claim on one we're going out with tomorrow," Cole replied with a shrug. "You'll have to find your own girl."

"Yeah, another night of choosing from the Cove girls. That's a jerk move," a guy next to Bryce chimed in.

"This is Pierce," Cole explained, and he pointed to another guy as well, introducing him as Jet. I hoped that was just a nickname.

"So you guys all work together?" I asked, trying to make friendly conversation. It made sense they were friends with Cole – they all looked oddly similar. Broad chests, big biceps, and tattoos on all four of them.

"Yeah, we all grew up around here," Pierce explained, chugging down the rest of the beer in his bottle. "We all work at the bike shop."

"When Cole actually shows up," Bryce razzed him. "What's old Harvey got you running now? You're barely around these days."

"Eh, I don't know man, just some new people he's been working with," Cole shrugged. "He's got some new projects."

I wondered if these other guys knew about Harvey's business. Cole seemed vague, even with them.

"You guys want to head out rucking next weekend?" Pierce asked the guys. "You could join us if you want," he said politely towards me.

"I'm not sure I even know what that is," I replied embarrassedly.

"Sometimes on the weekends we get together with our packs and scale the mountains," Cole explained. "It's pretty fun, but exhausting.

I'll have to take you out for a beginner's course one of these days."

"Hey, this is my buddy Chad," Jet said to the group as another guy walked up and joined us. There was no way I would remember all of these names by the end of the night. Cole shook the new guy's hand and introduced himself, which led me to believe he was an outsider like me.

"Do you guys know each other?" Bryce gestured towards Chad and I. "He's a Ridge City guy too."

What on earth was a Ridge City guy? Yeah, I lived in Mountain Ridge, but no one ever referred to it as Ridge City if that's what he meant. This was the first I'd ever heard of that term, and it came up more than once tonight.

"Oh yeah? I'm in the graduate program at MRU," Chad said towards me with a smile.

"I just graduated from there in May," I replied. "Vet science."

"Really? I'm in the MBA program, I'm working on a tech startup," he continued.

"Cole!" shouted a voice from across the way. "Let's unload the truck!" I couldn't even see the guy yelling since he was pretty far back from the fire.

"Will you be fine for a sec?" Cole asked me courteously. Bryce and Pierce and Jet all looked like they were going with him.

"How many kegs did he bring?" Jet asked throwing up his hands. "I already helped him with one earlier. Do you want to come up with us Chad?"

"I'm not really a heavy lifter," he commented, gesturing towards his body. He was skinny and only about five-foot-eleven, looking like a runt next to the others. I laughed at his self deprecating humor.

"Stay here," Cole said politely towards me. "Jet, stay here too," Cole ordered. He turned and left with Pierce and Bryce to head towards the parking lot.

"Always the protector," Jet said, sounding a bit annoyed. "Hang tight, I need another drink." Jet walked away and it was just Chad and I left for forced awkward conversation this time.

"So how do you know these guys? You may be the only other one from MRU here," I said to Chad.

"Yeah, these guys are a trip. I have a BMW 1300 series, a motorcycle, and it broke down out this way the other day. Jet was awesome, he fixed it right up for me and we got to talking. The receptionist was flirting with me and somehow I got invited here," Chad explained. "I wasn't going to come, but they seem like pretty cool guys. And honestly the girl was cute, so that enticed me. I don't know though, it seems like a whole different world out here, right?"

"Why do they keep calling us Ridge City people? I've never even heard that before," I said, shaking my head. "We live like ten minutes away from them."

"I know, and it's the way they say it too, like they're repulsed. They hear you go to MRU and they have to act overly unimpressed. Yes, mock me for having an education, that's brilliant," he stated with a laugh. I totally understood what he was saying.

A group of girls passed us, staring us both down.

"Who are they?" one of the girls asked in a stuck-up tone.

"That's Cole's LC," another replied with a visible eye roll as they passed. "I don't know who that guy is, but Cole's gonna beat his ass when he sees him talking to her." They giggled and kept walking.

"What's an LC?" I asked offensively to Chad as the girls walked away. "They keep saying it, and it doesn't sound nice."

"I have no idea," he replied. "But your boyfriend isn't seriously going to kick my ass, right?" He almost sounded a bit nervous, which made me laugh.

"No," I began, "and I'm not sure he's technically even my boyfriend. But he's not that kind of guy anyway, I don't know why they're saying that."

Jet rejoined us, bringing me a red cup filled with something. It was a nice gesture so I accepted it, even though I had no plans on drinking it.

Chad and Jet talked about some of the girls, and Jet planned to wingman for him once the receptionist showed up. Finally Cole came back, carrying two plastic cups in his hands.

"You already have a drink?" he asked curiously, staring at the container in my hand.

"Yeah, Jet brought it over," I said politely. "Thank you by the way."

"This one is better," Cole said, handing me a new cup with a wink. He grabbed the other one from me and poured it out into the sand.

"That was a fresh beer man, what are you doing?" Jet said, sounding completely offended.

"Come on, there are a few other people I want you to meet," Cole said sweetly, putting an arm around my shoulders. We started walking towards another group of six or seven guys. "Try it," he suggested as we walked, gesturing towards the cup in my hand. "I figured it out."

"Figured what out?" I questioned, oblivious to what he was talking about.

"Your drink. I solved it," he said, sounding proud of himself.

I took a small sip, smiling as soon as it hit my lips. "Yes you did," I grinned. "Where did you get this?"

"Someone up in the parking lot had a bar out of their tailgate," he snickered. "Sprite and grenadine, right? No alcohol?"

"Yeah," I responded, still smiling. I thought back to two minutes ago when those mean girls suggested Cole would fight someone just for talking to me, while in reality, he seemed so far away from that type of guy. He was gone making me a Shirley Temple for Pete's sake.

We made it to the next group of people and Cole introduced me collectively to them all at once. They were all guys he played beach volleyball with once a week. They all politely said hello and said kind things to me, encouraging me to come down and watch a game sometime. They all seemed really nice and cordial. It seemed the guys around here had far better manners than the girls. I was interested to learn that Cole even played volleyball, he didn't really strike me as a team sports kind of guy. This seemed like good progress, learning these things about him. After some small talk, he excused us from the group.

"Do you want to walk down by the water?" he asked once we were alone. He held onto my hand and a shiver coursed through me as I thought back to the last time we held hands on the beach, when his lips were pressed against mine.

"Yes," I said eagerly. "I have some questions for you." I glanced over at him and he had a huge smile on his face.

"It's barely after ten," he remarked, looking down at his watch. "It's nowhere close to midnight."

"That's not what I mean," I said playfully. "What are all those girls calling me? A Ridge City LC or something? What is that?"

"Don't let them bother you, they're harmless," he explained, leading me down to the water's edge. We kicked off our sandals and set down our cups.

"They've been whispering about me all night," I retorted.

"They're jealous," he said with a slight laugh. "I literally heard them talking about the guy's name on your shoes for like ten minutes while we unloaded the kegs."

I glanced down at the old pair of sandals I just laid on the beach. There was a small Michael Kors label on the back. "Why do they care about my shoes?" I exclaimed. "What could they possibly have to say about that?"

"A lot, that's all I heard them talk about," he smirked. "They're girls. That's just something else for them to judge you for."

"So then what's a Ridge City LC?"

We walked up to an area of the beach where there were huge boulders. They were massive, sitting right up against the water's edge. We stopped walking and he turned to face me. The glow of the fire in the background didn't provide us with much light, but the full moon did. He looked at me with sweet eyes.

"Everyone from the Mountain Ridge side is considered a Ridge City, that's just what people around here call them," he explained, both my hands in his now that we stopped walking.

"And the LC part?" I urged.

"It's just a dumb expression, it stands for loose change," he said, shaking his head. "It's stupid."

"I don't get it," I replied curiously. No wonder it hadn't taken off and appeared to just be a West Cove thing.

"I don't really know, it kind of has several meanings," he said, cocking his head back. "Guys usually mean it in the context of seeing a girl at a bar or a party or a nightclub or something. Like he wants to check her pockets for loose change… It's dumb, it just means he wants to put his hands all over her or whatever. Girls use it differently though, like an insult."

"And the guy version isn't insulting?" I asked dryly.

"I know, but for girls it's more like a cast aside. Like how every once in a while you need loose change, but for the most part you don't, it just gets in the way… Or like how people throw change into a fountain," he tried to explain. "It's like they're trying to say loose change isn't important or significant or whatever."

"And they got that impression of me from my sandals?" I said lightheartedly, trying not to let it bother me. I couldn't help it though, these were Cole's 'people.' I obviously wanted to be accepted by them in some way.

"Let them judge you however they want, it doesn't mean anything," he said sweetly, bringing up one of his hands to touch my face.

"What about you?" I asked apprehensively. "I'm sure you see a Ridge City girl too when you look at me. I get it."

"You know what I actually see? What I saw in you from the first night I met you?" he said softly. "*Goodness*. It's the most fascinating thing to me, the way it just pours out of you. I've never seen that in someone the way I see it in you." He slowly grazed his lips against mine.

"I'm not so good," I said quietly.

"That's just it," he replied, gently brushing my cheek with his hand as he touched my face. "You are, in every single way, but it's like you don't know how much it stands out on you. I honestly didn't know that kind of goodness even existed before you. You're like a dream I never knew to have."

He kissed me again, more passionately this time, and his words filled me. I didn't honestly believe I was any more or less ordinary than anyone else I knew. I was who I was, but the way he saw me through his eyes – that was something far more than ordinary. Kind of the way his presence felt to me – not just because he was physically so big and strong, but the fierceness in his voice when he wanted to protect me from something – that burned through me and I felt cared for in a way I never recognized before.

His arms wrapped tight around me, and I was entranced by his embrace. It felt sturdy and powerful, but also delicate and tender in some way.

He trailed kisses down my neck and my entire body felt it. I wrapped my arms around him, reveling in the moment.

Loud shouts from around the bonfire echoed out through the quiet night, breaking our concentration on each other. We both looked over to see what the noise was. It appeared to be a couple guys fighting.

"Of course, something else to go wrong tonight," he said with a sigh and a hint of frustration.

"This night hasn't been so bad," I replied with a sexy smirk, turning his attention back on me.

"No? What was the highlight for you?" he asked with an amused look on his face.

"Earlier, when you stopped the truck," I said hesitantly, not totally sure I was ready to share my honest thoughts with him just yet.

"Stopping for Crazy Jamie was the best part?" he replied gregariously, throwing his hands up in the air with a laugh. "See, that's what I'm talking about. Only you would say that."

"That's not the part I was referencing," I said with a shy smile. "When you approached her…" I said reluctantly. "You called me your girl."

"That was your highlight?" he said with a boyish grin. I nodded. "Good," he whispered. "Then I'll keep saying it."

He kissed me again, completely ignoring our surroundings and anything happening over by the fire. It was as if we were the only people out under the night sky. His strong arms wrapped around me again and scooped me up so that my legs were straddling him. He leaned us up against one of the rocks and our bodies were completely pressed up against each other. His lips searched mine, moving downward as I held onto him.

"Seriously, blink twice and I'll carry you out of here," he whispered into my hair as his hands slid down the contours of my body.

I looked up at the stars hovering perfectly above us. I knew with complete certainty in this moment that whatever secrets Cole had, big or not, they didn't matter to me. If they didn't change the way he felt about me, or the way he saw me, then I didn't care. If we could be together – if I could feel like this – cared for, safe, protected, wanted….

Then nothing else mattered.

CHAPTER 9

Sunlight filtered in through the sides of my bedroom curtains as I stirred and rolled over. The clock read nine-thirty which was impressive for me, even for a weekend. I never slept this late. I thought back to everything that had happened the night before – Cole's hands – our bodies pressed up against each other... I stared at him lying next to me, shirtless and asleep.

I had to admit, I never really understood the whole tattoo thing, especially when people had them all over their bodies. Cole had more than I thought, not just on his biceps, but across his entire upper back. I vaguely remembered a few on his chest as well from the night before. Staring at him now though, it didn't seem strange to me at all. Instead he looked like a perfectly painted canvas, like a complete work of art. It made him beautiful to me.

I climbed out of bed, putting on his grey v-neck shirt lying on the floor. It practically looked like a dress on me. I tiptoed to the kitchen and opened my fridge, wondering what I had to make us breakfast. Unfortunately the fridge sound alerted Dexter, and he went nuts for his own breakfast. I quickly set a bowl of pellets in front of him, hoping he didn't wake up Cole. I quietly walked back upstairs to check and see if he was still sleeping. As soon as I entered the room, he smiled at me.

"It actually happened," he said with a grin. "You really are a bad friend, you literally borrowed my clothes without asking."

I climbed onto the bed with a sultry look. "You gave me your expressed permission to borrow them anytime I wanted, remember?"

I leaned down and kissed him softly. He grabbed my sides, making me giggle, and pulled me next to him.

I traced the tattoos on his chest, finally making a point to actually look at them. "What's this, *413*?" I asked, pointing to one above his heart.

"Here we go," he replied, smiling at me. "Now I have to answer every question you ask of me, right? All of a sudden, now that you're my girl, I can't just shrug you off any more?"

"Nope," I giggled, lying down right next to him. "Start talking."

"That's the day Harvey became my legal guardian," he stated, almost looking embarrassed to be talking about it. "April thirteenth."

"Why no year on there?" I wondered aloud.

"Because that part is unimportant," he explained. "That day changed me, for the better obviously. But it didn't matter to me whether it was five years ago, or fifteen years ago… It's the day that mattered."

"So what about that one," I said pointing to another tattoo with an *818* on it. I assumed that was an important date as well.

"That's the day God sent me back here," he said, staring at me with an honest expression. "I was in a pretty bad motorcycle accident. I still have some scars here," he said, pointing to areas on his chest and around his ribs. I touched them gently with my fingertips. "I was pronounced dead at the scene. Then I took a breath." He shrugged like that was it, but I imagined it was a much bigger moment.

"Do you remember it actually happening?" I questioned, wanting to know more.

"No, people ask me that all the time, if I saw lights or whatever. Honestly I don't remember a single thing, I woke up out of a coma three days later and someone had to tell me what happened. But I don't know, I felt changed after that. Something must've happened. They told me I shouldn't have gotten a second chance, but that breath… I wouldn't know how else to explain it."

I smiled at him as he spoke. I loved listening to him open up to me. Things had certainly changed between us after last night.

"What really happened here?" I asked softly, running my finger along his left forearm, the area I cleaned and put back together the night we first met. He finally took the bandage off it yesterday and I could see the wound was healing well.

"Harvey runs some kind of gambling circuit," he began, not hesitating this time to tell me the story. "Usually he handles it all himself, but this time he was working for another guy. I never met him, someone named Waltz or something like that, probably his last name. Harvey couldn't cover one of the bets, which isn't usually a risk he takes, so I don't know where it fell apart that night, honestly. But Harvey went out to try and handle one of the drops himself, and he was shorting the guy some money. I don't know why he didn't send someone else to do it, that was a red flag to me. That's usually the kind of work I do for him. I mean I'm not out ripping people off. But when he owes money or when someone owes him, I collect it."

"It's all from gambling?" I clarified, trying to understand what he was telling me. I knew Mountain Ridge had plenty of casinos, but I knew nothing about gambling outside of one.

"No," he answered honestly. "There's other stuff."

I appreciated his truthfulness, but I could tell by his hesitation that we were at a point he didn't want to continue with the details.

"And you've been stabbed before over this kind of thing?" I asked, trying to redirect the conversation. I guess it didn't matter where the money was from, it didn't sound legal either way.

"Sometimes we get roughed up a bit, it happens," he confirmed. "But usually he doesn't send me for those, he's got some other guys who deal with most of those jobs. They're a lot rougher than me."

"I think you were right before, maybe I don't want to know more," I conceded, starting to feel worried about him. I had a pit in my stomach, and I hated the feeling. Instead I preferred pretending Cole was more oblivious to Harvey's activities than what he was now sharing with me.

"So no further questions?" he asked with a smirk.

"Just one more," I said, not totally sure I wanted to bring it up now. But while he was being so forthcoming and honest with me, I figured it was a good time to get it off my chest. "Who's Britt?"

"Oh no, now it's getting good," he said, laying flat on his back with a laugh. "It's easier for me to talk about now, but it was a rough situation for awhile. How do you know about her?"

"I saw her at the party last night, and one of your friends told me who she was. I didn't get any details though," I explained, sitting up to look at him. "Any tattoos of her?" I studied his chest, but the rest of the designs were more like art that I couldn't decipher.

"This one was supposed to be," he said rolling over, pointing to a spot over his shoulder. "Not for her exactly, but for the baby's birth date."

"You have a baby?" I gasped, suddenly regretting this entire topic. I hadn't even considered something like that. I had hoped for some crazy high school sweetheart montage, not something more serious than that.

"That's the kicker," he said, burying his face in his hands. "We dated on and off in high school, but she couldn't keep out of the guy's locker room," he said with some sarcastic irritation. "I swear she slept with half the football team while we were together."

"Why did you stay with her?"

"I didn't know better," he said speculatively. "I was a dumb eighteen year old kid. She knew about me, she knew about my situation with my parents and Harvey and stuff. So it was just… comfortable. She made me feel like she was the best I could ever do, and I believed that."

He looked at me with such honest eyes, and I felt sad for him for a moment. It seemed like he never had a real, true relationship in his life, as a child or even as an adult.

"She got pregnant when we were twenty, so I figured that was it. Maybe that would settle her down and we could try the family thing. I don't know. Things were even rocky then when it was supposed to be good news. It was a toxic relationship. She continued to remind me that was the best it could ever get for me, and I drowned myself in shadowing Harvey, trying to pick up business for him so I could earn extra money to support a family."

"I feel like this story has a sad ending," I said softly.

"Quite the opposite," he said with a smirk, rubbing his forehead. "The baby came out a whole lot darker than my summer tan."

I clasped my hands over my mouth. I couldn't believe that kind of thing actually happened to people.

"Seriously?" I stated loudly.

"Well needless to say I never filled in the birth date on the tattoo," he said with an embarrassing blush. "Yeah, I was that guy at the hospital waiting for my kid to be born, just to find out I didn't have a kid being born. It was mortifying."

"So that was it? You finally realized you should be done with her?"

"Yep, that was the turning point," he said with a slight laugh. "I felt like such an idiot. For a year or two after, every so often when she had a break from yet another failed relationship, she would come around, but I was numb to it by then. Sadly it took something that traumatizing for me to realize she wasn't the girl for me."

I was still amazed by this entire conversation, but relieved at the same time. When he told me initially he had secrets, I thought those secrets were more along the lines of, you know, *murder* or something. This was far easier to handle.

"*She* was judging me up and down last night as not being good enough for you, and *that's* what she put you through?"

"I know, she's a peach, right?" he laughed. "I was messed up for awhile of course after that. As if I didn't already have trust issues before then, that certainly didn't help. So, I've just focused on work and southern California ever since."

"You'll really leave here?" I said feeling somewhat saddened by the thought. I knew all of this was so new, Cole and I. It's not like I could hold him back from any of that. I just hoped his plans were much farther out in the future.

"I'm still saving up," he said hesitantly. "Land in California isn't cheap. But I think I'll be ready for it sooner than later." He looked at me sweetly as he said it. "Do you want to go with me willingly, or will I have to kidnap you like we talked about earlier?"

"How did we get from tacos to California in just a few days?" I laughed. Obviously I knew he was kidding. No one would be so crazy.

"You obviously don't watch much baseball," he teased. "After home plate is California. That's how it works."

I playfully smacked his arm and he pulled me in close to him. He caressed my face, and all the tingles I had before surged back through my body.

We spent the rest of the morning wrapped up in my sheets, and I felt like nothing could wipe the stupid grin off my face. He was so different from everything I first imagined the night we met. I was obviously drawn to his handsome face initially, that was impossible not to notice. But the way he spoke to me – he was so full of sincerity and genuine concern and he was more thoughtful than I ever imagined he would be. And then there was the way he touched me, with such tenderness – I was initially so intimidated by him, but I knew now with certainty that these hands of his would never be unkind to me. They held me with such purpose, and I was so eager to begin this adventure with him. After Ian, that feeling of falling I couldn't escape from – like my arms were flailing around but unable to ever pull my weight up – Cole's arms caught me in the midst of all that.

I knew it was far too soon to tell where this was going, or how this would end. I wasn't so naïve to think this was my happy ever after, I knew that in itself was a rarity, and not everyone even got that kind of ending. But whatever this was, it was already changing me into the girl I was before my mistake – before my hesitation and uncertainty as to what I wanted – and I knew I would be forever changed by meeting Cole Mason. Maybe our time together would be brief, or maybe it would be so much more than that. Either way, what I felt now – it was a whole different kind of falling.

CHAPTER 10

Cole and I finally managed to separate our bodies from each other and he left around lunchtime to go get the boat. He simply said he was borrowing it from a friend, but didn't offer more details than that. I was going to pick up Sam and we were all going to meet up at the docks around two.

When I pulled into Sam's apartment lot, she ran outside before I even had time to get out of the car. She was wearing a white cotton swimsuit cover dress over her bright pink bikini. Her hair was perfectly smooth as it framed her face and her lips were a light pink. She looked adorable, and the ginormous smile spread across her mouth certainly helped.

"I am so excited for this," she gushed as she climbed into my small silver SUV. "You have to catch me up on everything before we get there. What's going on with you and Cole? You're beaming right now, plus you haven't been texting me, so I'm guessing you've spent some more time with him?"

I filled her in on everything that had happened between us, and she was genuinely happy for me. She squealed excitedly as she realized this was officially our first time double dating.

"For that to have happened before, I would've had to go out with Brandt when you were dating Ian," she commented with a scrunched up face. "Can you imagine that?"

Brandt was such a nice, sweet guy, but he and Sam never would've worked together. He was far from her type.

"So wait, you said you saw Luke at the bonfire, right? Any info for me? How did he seem? Was he talking to other girls?" Sam questioned.

I tried thinking back to my time with him, even though honestly that wasn't one of the events my mind was fixated on. "He was really polite," I started, trying to think of kind things to say. "He seems like a decent guy. I'm still not sure about the direction of their music," I smirked. "You'll have to get more out of him on that. But I didn't see him hitting on anyone else or anything. I would hope he's not dumb enough to do that in front of your best friend, but I guess you never know."

We followed the signs to the parking lot for the boat docks and I saw Cole's truck was already there. He was dressed in bright green swim shorts and a thin white t-shirt, and he was wearing a baseball hat which I'd never seen him in before. He looked sexy as hell in it; more laid back than he usually did. Luke was wearing red shorts and a grey tank top similar to the one he wore at the bar the other night. They were standing outside of the truck, waiting on us.

As soon as we parked and exited my car, Cole scooped me up and kissed me like it had been days since we'd last seen each other, even though it had been less than two hours. I loved everything about the butterflies in my stomach as he held me. He kissed my lips one more time and then set me down.

"I feel like I need to up the dramatics on my hello," Luke said towards Sam, gesturing towards Cole and I. We all laughed at his remark.

"The boat's already in and loaded, let's head out," Cole said, wrapping an arm around my shoulders. Sam and I both grabbed our beach bags and the guys helped us on to a decent-sized pontoon boat. It was definitely too big for just the four of us, but I didn't care. I was looking forward to our afternoon in the sun together. Sam's grin suggested she was also excited for this escapade.

Cole skillfully drove the boat out and away from the docks, and I imagined he had a lot of experience in doing so.

"Is this boat yours?" Sam asked Cole as Luke slid closer to her on one of the bench seats. "This is awesome."

"It belongs to a friend of mine," Cole explained, driving us out to the middle of the lake. "He keeps it on Harvey's lot, where I stay, so he lets me use it whenever I want. It's pretty easy to hook up to the truck, so me and the guys try to head out here maybe once a month or so."

"I love this, I would love to have a boat," I chimed in, staring out at the water. It was so perfectly blue it was mesmerizing.

"My girl wants a boat now?" he said sarcastically, keeping his eyes out towards the water. "I'm gonna need to pick up some extra shifts at the bike shop to make that happen," he teased. "Maybe we can just borrow this one for awhile to see if it really suits us." He cut the engine and the boat slowed and wobbled in the water.

"That works for me too," I replied, walking up behind and wrapping my arms around his waist.

"Do you guys want to go for a swim?" Cole asked.

Sam and I nodded our heads at the same time, and Luke also agreed. Sam and I slid our bags over and took off our swim cover-ups. My bikini was red with white polka dots and I was thankful for all the laying out Sam and I did so that I already had a great tan going.

Luke opened a cooler, digging through it for a drink. I motioned towards Sam with my head and I swear, like so many times before, she could read my mind. She reached out and grabbed my hand and we ran down the length of the boat, doing cannonballs together into the cold water.

As we surfaced, the guys were leaning over the boat, staring at us.

"You girls are crazy," Luke said with a smile, shaking his head. He turned towards the center of the boat and peeled off his grey tank top. "I'm gonna love this girl," he said towards Cole. Sam blushed as she overheard the comment.

"We can't let them show us up," Cole stated matter-of-factly. "You ready?" Both of them turned and ran off the end of the boat just as we had, leaping right over us. Their giant splashes covered us with water. Cole quickly swam up to me and wiped the water off my face. He kissed me tenderly.

"Are you guys going to be sucking face all day?" Sam said, splashing us with water.

I smiled, unable to keep the happiness from radiating through me.

"Let's grab a drink," Luke suggested, motioning back up on the boat. He helped Sam up the small ladder attached to the back of the boat and they started talking. I couldn't make out their conversation though. Cole and I swam through the water, and it felt perfectly refreshing on such a hot July day.

"So what do you think? I know you don't know Sam at all, but is this a good match up?" I asked Cole as we floated in the water. "You at least know a little bit about Luke."

"He's a West Cove guy. I'm sure he's more than happy to be here with a girl like that right now," Cole said earnestly. "I've known Tyler forever, he's a decent guy. But I didn't know Luke until they formed the band. That was maybe six months ago?" he estimated. "From what I can tell he seems okay, but he knows some pretty shady people."

"Well for you to know them, then you must know those same shady people, right? To know that they're shady in the first place?" I mused.

"Good point," he snickered. "But I know not to trust them. He seems to be quite friendly with them, so that's the difference. All I know is that they have some business with Harvey, which usually isn't a good thing. Luke doesn't seem to be involved, but the fact that his close friends are, that's not a great sign. But I guess he's worth a chance if she ends up really liking him."

"If doing business with Harvey is so bad, then why are you involved?" I asked, trying to figure it all out. It seemed like quite the contradiction.

"It all depends on what side of Harvey's business you're on," he vaguely explained. "Technically I work *with* Harvey. They work *for* him. That's where the difference comes into play."

"I feel like I never understand what you're actually saying," I sighed, feeling like I never got anywhere when we talked about his work.

"Maybe it's because you're love-struck," he teased, changing the subject. "You don't understand it because you're too mesmerized by me to stay focused on the details. I swear I've given you so many clear, uncomplicated details…" He wrapped an arm around my waist under the water, using his other arm to grab the side of the boat to steady us.

"Every time we talk about it, you give me *no* details, and then you get all sweet and handsy with me and I forget about it," I replied, touching his face. "Just promise me it's nothing that will get you in any trouble." I guess at the end of the day I didn't care what he really did. But when he hinted that Harvey's business wasn't totally legal, I couldn't help but worry about him a bit. And the violence – that wasn't my thing at all.

"You're going to get me in far more trouble than anything else could," he said seductively, kissing me up against the boat.

We continued swimming for a bit and I couldn't help but notice that Sam and Luke seemed to be getting along well on the boat. They were sitting closely together, presumably talking, and I could hear Sam's infectious laugh intermittently which led me to believe she was enjoying herself.

Cole and I eventually climbed back on board and joined them. We listened to some music and took in the balmy sunshine. It was such a relaxing afternoon without a care in the world. Cole got a phone call around five-thirty and he didn't talk much, but someone on the other end must've given him some frustrating news. His face changed as he listened in. He looked irritated by something, and I hoped it wouldn't change his mood for the rest of the day.

"Is everything okay?" I asked with concern as soon as he hung up the phone.

"Everything will be fine," he said with a reassuring tone. The look on his face made me think he was trying to convince himself of that more so than me. "Are you guys hungry? I know a good spot we can drive the boat to for some grub."

"That sounds wonderful," Sam said happily. "Hey Syd, will you go back to Local Joe's with me next week? Luke has another show on Wednesday."

I looked over at Cole who was directing the boat towards the shoreline across from where we were at. I knew I didn't need his permission to go, but I respected the fact that he would probably want to join us.

"What are you looking at me for?" he asked with a laugh, picking up on my expression. "You don't need to ask me, you can go with your best friend wherever want. I'm never gonna be the guy who tells you otherwise."

"I thought you told me I shouldn't go back?" I questioned.

"Not alone," he answered with a smirk. "So you can either ask me to join you guys, which I would politely accept, or leave me out of it - in which case I'll be standing in a dark corner. Either way, I'm good with whatever you want to do. Relationships are all about compromise, right?" I laughed as he shrugged his shoulders.

"So either way you're going," I clarified, studying his face.

"Cole is right on that," Luke interjected. "You girls shouldn't ever be alone there. I mean yeah, I'm technically there, but I can't keep track of you while I'm on stage. It's not a good place. Last year Cole, what, four separate girls went missing from there? That was the last place they were ever seen."

"Seriously?" I replied, caught off guard by the fact it was *that* bad. "Why don't you just explain it that way, Cole? That's enough to make me beg you to go with us."

"I don't want to sound like a crazy overprotective guy," Cole replied. "I know you're getting that impression from me, and I genuinely don't mean to do it. I'm not possessive or jealous or whatever, you always have a choice whether or not you want to be with me. But if your choice is to *be* with me, you're crazy if you think I'll let you hang out in West Cove without me being around. A lot of crazy stuff happens around there, and it doesn't all get reported on the news."

Cole guided the boat up along a set of docks outside a cute little beach restaurant. There were string lights hung up all around and we could smell hamburgers cooking as soon as we headed off the boat.

"How cute is this place?" Sam asked excitedly. Luke grabbed her hand as we walked towards the restaurant and I knew she was smitten.

We were seated at a table overlooking the water and we had fun conversation throughout the meal. We learned a little more about Luke. He worked part time at a restaurant but spent most of his time sending demos out to record labels. He genuinely loved music and wanted so badly to make it big. He knew Soul Punch wasn't going to get him there, but it at least made him a little money on the side and he was able to work on his music. Sam got along so well with Cole which made me happy. He was so charismatic and funny, and I loved that side of him. Yeah, he seemed a little too protective at times, but when I really gave it some thought – how he grew up, where he came from – it at least seemed justified to me.

After dinner we made our way back to the boat and headed back across the lake to the docks where Cole's truck was parked. We laughed and listened to loud music, Sam and I dancing together when one of our favorite songs came on. It was such a perfect summer day, and I loved every minute of it. Sam and Luke talked about heading out for a drink when we got back and they asked if we wanted to join them. We happily agreed.

Cole maneuvered the boat up to the dock and helped us get off. "Why don't you guys head back to your place and get cleaned up? Luke can help me load the boat back up and we'll drop it off at the warehouse. We'll come pick you guys up in around thirty minutes or so?"

Sam and I nodded. It would be nice to change out of our swimsuits and cover-ups for something more nighttime-date worthy. Cole leaned in and kissed me sweetly while Sam and Luke rolled their eyes at us. We parted ways and Sam and I headed back to my place.

"So, how was it with Luke? Give me details," I interrogated her now that we were alone. I could tell by the huge grin on her face that it went well.

"He's totally not my type," she gushed, "but I don't care. He's so handsome. And his voice is all deep and raspy like a musician… I mean he is one, even though he doesn't sing in Soul Punch. I know it's so dumb to be falling for a band guy with no ambition. But I only have until next month anyway before I head to Oregon. So this is exactly what I need."

"And then you'll just move away and that's that, even if you fall for him?" I asked curiously. Sam seemed realistic enough to realize this was just a summer fling before she moved away, but she also cared deeply for people. I wondered if she would be able to handle the end of it as easily as she thought she could.

"I don't know, maybe we can be long distance pen pals," she teased. "I know, it probably seems like a waste of my time. But think about it, how much time can we spend together between now and then? I'm at the clinic several full days a week, plus my summer school classes… So we're talking like ten dates probably. It's not like I'll fall in love with him. We can just have fun and whatever."

Yeah, like it was ever that easy.

"What about you and Cole? I thought he wasn't your type? And then I see you guys together and you're inseparable, like you've known each other a lot longer," she stated, shifting the focus onto me.

"I know, I don't know what it is," I said honestly. "You know I don't rush into things. Ian asked me out for what, like a month before we even went on our first date? I tried brushing Cole off originally, you know that. But it's weird, I just can't get him out of my head. I can't stop thinking about him when we're not together. He just has this presence."

"I knew it, you're falling," she said candidly.

"Not after a week, come on. That's too quick," I replied.

"Sometimes it happens like that," she shrugged. "I see the way he looks at you. It's so intense. It's different."

"What do you mean by *different*?" I asked, interested in her opinion.

"Ian adored you, that was so obvious. When he looked at you, you could tell he was smitten. He was in awe of you, and he cared deeply for you. You could tell by his eyes. But Cole looks at you in a different way. I don't know, he just has this fierceness in his eyes like he would do anything in the world for you. It's like he's afraid you're just passing through, like you're just a dream or something, and he looks like he so desperately wants to hold onto you no matter the circumstances."

Her words made so much sense in a way, which surprised me since she didn't know the things I knew about him. She didn't know about his past or his family. The crazy thing was, I had no intentions of falling in love at all, and certainly not with a guy like Cole. But the way he looked at me sometimes – Sam was right, there was so much in his eyes. He had this protective, passionate way of just consuming me with his stare. I knew it would be harder and harder to resist as time passed.

We made it back to my apartment and quickly got cleaned up. Since Sam had on her swim suit originally when we met up, she borrowed some of my clothes for the night out. We each put on a light summer dress and casual sandals and we fixed our makeup. A few minutes after we were ready, there was a knock on my door. I knew it was Luke knocking, because Cole's knock was always so much more gentle. It seemed like a strange thing to notice, but I did.

Sam opened the door and sure enough, there was Luke, with Cole right behind him. They escorted us out to Cole's truck and we climbed in.

"Some friends of mine are playing at Smokey's," Luke announced, suggesting we head there. "Does that sound okay?"

"Can't we take them to a Ridge bar? Somewhere nicer?" Cole recommended.

"It'll be a killer show," Luke said persuasively. "I think you guys would like it."

"Sounds fun," Sam said excitedly, obviously willing to go wherever he wanted. Cole looked over at me and I shrugged, suggesting I was up for anything.

"Fine," Cole said, pulling the truck out from in front of my condo. He did a U-turn and headed west. I assumed from the way we were driving, this was going to be another West Cove dive bar special.

We pulled into the lot of a bar called Smokey's and it looked awfully similar to Local Joe's. It was definitely run down and in desperate need of some work. The parking lot was busy and we could hear the music inside from the parking lot.

We all headed indoors and I wasn't surprised to find that it was smoky and pretty tiny. The place was mostly full of young guys, very much into the rock music playing from a small stage, but there were a few girls in there as well. A few of them looked vaguely familiar – I assumed I recognized them from the bonfire last night, but they didn't look any more friendly tonight.

"I'll get us some drinks," Cole said as we all stood towards the back of the room. The music was so loud that I knew it was going to be hard to have any conversation in here. Luke looked really into the music though, so I imagine he wanted to stay. And Sam looked really into Luke, so that pretty much confirmed we'd be staying here for the night.

Cole brought back two beers for him and Luke, a cranberry vodka for Sam, and my usual cherry Sprite. I appreciated that he never made a big deal out of the fact that I didn't drink. We didn't even talk about it, but after everything I'd told him about Ian, I figured he respected my reasoning for it. He looked around the room, taking everyone in. He had a suspicious expression on his face, but then again, he had that same look at Local Joe's. It's like he was forever assessing every person in the room.

The current band ended and another one came on stage to set up their equipment.

"These are my buddies," Luke said with a grin. "Do you want to move closer?" Sam happily nodded and he grabbed her hand and they moved towards the front of the stage.

"Do you mind if we hang back here?" Cole asked politely.

"I would prefer it," I said honestly. The music just playing was loud and crappy, and I wasn't overly optimistic for the next band. I had no desire to be closer to it with sweaty drunk guys all up against me. I imaged Cole would be happier that way as well. While the music was on hiatus, I took advantage of the quiet and made conversation with Cole.

"I have an idea," I said suggestively.

"And if you keep that look on your face while you ask me, I will say yes, to whatever it is," he replied with a smirk.

"Well you already stayed at my place last night. Can we stay at yours tonight? I mean, assuming you weren't planning on just dropping me off at home alone," I said with a sexy grin.

"I definitely wasn't planning to drop you off alone tonight," he answered, wrapping an arm around my waist. "But why would you want to stay at my place? It's not nearly as nice as yours."

"I don't care how nice it is," I stated honestly. "I just want to see it. I want to see your world. I want to know where you stay."

"It's that important to you?"

"Yes. If we're going to be together, I want to know everything about you," I said sincerely.

He smiled down at me, shaking his head. "You are so hard to say no to." He kissed me slowly and then pulled back, still keeping a hand on my face. "Do we have to do it tonight? I feel like I just need more time. I have to know it won't change your mind about me. It's just where I live, it's not who I am."

It was sad to me that he thought I would become uninterested in him over what his house looked like. Surely he knew deep down that I wasn't that shallow. I didn't care about houses or motorcycles or *things.* I cared about him. That was it.

Loud music started up and our conversation was cut short. I could tell he wasn't ready to bring me into his world just yet. He didn't even want me going to bars near where he lived, so I suppose it made sense he wasn't eager to show me where he stayed.

This next band instantly sounded better than the last one, and I wondered why Luke wasn't playing with these guys instead if they were friends of his. They sounded much more in tune with each other.

As the band played, I noticed a group of three guys walking towards Cole and I. They looked like they recognized him, but they didn't look happy to see him. Cole must've noticed them at the same time I did. He reached down for my hand and squeezed it.

"Where's your old man tonight?" a stocky guy with a shaved head said above the music towards Cole as he approached.

"Not here," Cole responded curtly. "I have no business with you."

"Well I have plenty of unfinished business with you," he sneered. "Let's head outside. Now."

CHAPTER 11

Cole looked down at me and I couldn't read his expression. He didn't look worried like I would expect – but he definitely looked irritated. I imagined I was in the way at this point, but I wasn't sure what to do. I tried to find Sam and Luke in the crowd by the stage, but there were so many people that I couldn't make them out.

"I'm not looking for any trouble tonight," Cole said straightforwardly.

"I can see that," the bald guy said with a low whistle, looking me up and down.

"Tommy, leave her out of this, I swear," Cole said sternly.

"I can't even imagine the sweet lies you have to tell in order to get a girl like this to run around with a lowlife like you," Tommy replied.

"Leave my girl out of this," Cole said again, gritting his teeth. "Walk away or I swear you will regret this."

"Does he talk tough like that to you in bed too, sweetheart?" Tommy snickered. The words were barely out of his mouth before Cole raised up a strong arm and clocked him in the face. I think I screamed.

Tommy continued to come at Cole, but Cole's unrelenting blows quickly sent him to the ground. Blood poured out of his face. The two other guys with Tommy joined in, one hitting Cole in the face and the other trying to pull Cole off of the bloody man on the ground.

"Cole, stop!" I shrieked. Tommy looked unresponsive, but Cole continued hitting hm. "Cole! Enough! Stop!"

The music kept screaming from the stage, as if this horrible bloody mess wasn't happening. Most eyes were oblivious to what was going on, although a few people were watching once they heard all of the commotion. Finally two large security guys from the bar came over and tried to break it up. Fists were still flying everywhere and I backed up as far as I could, not knowing where else to go. All I knew is that I so desperately wanted out of that room, but there were too many people. I felt like I was suffocating.

One of the security guys finally got Cole off of Tommy, and there was so much blood. Cole had blood on his face and all over his hands, and even some on his light blue t-shirt. Tears started pouring down my eyes, even though I couldn't get a handle on how I truly felt at the moment. The whole scene terrified me – the fists, the blood, the look in Cole's eyes.

My whole body felt like it was trembling as Cole was shoved outside of the bar. Tommy still laid on the ground and I heard people screaming to call 911. I stood against the wall, covering my mouth, hoping everything I just witnessed wasn't true.

Some guy in black clothes came and grabbed my arm, leading me towards the front of the bar. "You need to get out of here or he won't leave," the stranger said loudly into my ear. The band was still playing and I just wanted to scream at the top of my lungs. I wanted to scream until someone carried me out of here – until I was tucked under the covers of my own, warm bed. Alone.

The guy physically escorted me to the front and shoved me outside where Cole was pacing. "We have to go," he said in a firm voice.

"What the hell was that?" I hissed. "He didn't even do anything to you. You kept hitting him and he wasn't even fighting back. There was so much blood everywhere," I rambled, unsure how to compose myself. My hands were shaking so bad.

"I'm serious, we have about ninety seconds before the cops show up," he urged. He still had so much anger in his eyes, I swear I barely recognized him.

"I don't want to go with you," I said through my tears. I wanted to leave, that was true. These surroundings couldn't have felt more foreign to me. But the look in Cole's eyes, and the amount of blood all over him – I was petrified. I felt like I couldn't move.

"Syd, you have to," he said sternly. "I swear I'm going to carry you out of here if you don't start walking, the cops are coming!"

“Probably because you just beat the shit out of some guy who didn’t lay a hand on you,” I sneered. “What was that? This is not okay, Cole.”

He flexed his arms into fists and I could see the frustration rise in his eyes. “You can lecture me about this anywhere else,” he said through gritted teeth, “but not here. We have to go.” He picked me up in his strong arms, and I could feel the blood on him rubbing onto my bare skin. Tears continued to pour out of me.

“Put me down,” I sobbed, “I don’t want to go with you.”

“I’m not leaving you here,” he replied firmly. “If you refuse to come with me, I will get arrested and thrown in jail before I drive away without you in my truck. I refuse to leave you here.”

I wanted to continue arguing with him but he carried me to his truck anyway and I knew it was a conversation I would lose. He seemed to do whatever he wanted to anyway.

Sure enough, I could hear sirens in the distance. There was no doubt in my mind they were headed this way. Cole quickly opened the door of his truck and set me down on the seat, hurrying over to the driver’s side. He climbed in and started up the engine so fast, we were peeling out of the bar parking lot before I could even get my seatbelt on.

I had no idea where he was headed, but it sure wasn’t towards the downtown lights of

Mountain Ridge. I sat next to him, crying, unable to speak. He drove for three or four minutes up a dirt road, nestled back into the trees, then finally pulled over and parked the truck.

"Sydney," he began, running his fingers through his light brown hair, looking frustrated.

"Don't Cole," I said angrily through my tears. "I just want to go home."

"You can stay at my place tonight," he replied softly, as if him giving in on that made up for everything that just happened.

"I don't want to. I want to go home," I repeated.

"I thought you really wanted to stay with me?" he said quietly.

"Cole, you're covered in blood. That doesn't seem like a problem to you?" I said a little too loudly. I hated the way he made me feel like I was being irrational.

"That guy, he…"

"I don't want to hear about it," I cut him off, throwing up my hands and shaking my head. "I told you I wanted to know everything about you, I know that. But I don't. I don't want to know anything else about you." More tears poured out and I knew I wasn't going to get any stronger throughout this conversation. "Look at your fists. Do you realize what they just did?"

He looked down at his swollen, bloody fists. Both of them looked twice the size. The cut on his forearm, the one from the night we met – it was opened back up, and blood poured out. His left cheek was also red and beginning to swell. “Syd, he’s not a good guy,” Cole began, as if such simple words could erase anything that just happened.

“And you are?” I asked unsympathetically.

“No,” he said quietly. “But I never told you I was.”

“I want to go home,” I said again, wishing I could just close my eyes and be somewhere else. “Please take me home.”

He stared into my wet eyes and the look on his face broke me. His eyes looked like I imaged they did as a twelve year old boy, when he realized no one was coming for him. He looked hurt and abandoned, like he just realized yet again that he had no one on his side.

“I’m sorry Syd, I really am. But please don’t look at me like that,” he begged, resting his arm on the steering wheel.

“Like what?”

“Like you’re afraid of me,” he said softly.

“Well I am,” I whispered as the tears continued. It was the truth. What I saw in him tonight – all that anger and rage he couldn’t seem to hold back – I didn’t know that was inside of him. It was truly terrifying.

“I would *never* hurt you, you have to believe that,” he pled, keeping his eyes on mine.

I leaned my head back and shut my eyes, unable to stare into his anymore – all the possibility I saw in them before was now gone.

"You already have," I whispered.

I leaned my head back and shut my eyes, unable to stare into his anymore. All the possibilities I saw in them before was now gone.

"You already have," I whispered.

CHAPTER 12

I thought I would struggle to fall asleep, or worse, I feared I would toss and turn all night from bad dreams of what happened at the bar. Instead, I awoke around nine a.m., feeling somewhat refreshed, even though my eyes were still swollen from all the crying the night before.

Cole dropped me off after our conversation in his truck last night, and I didn't say another word to him. He told me he wasn't leaving me as I got out of the truck, but he didn't make a move to get out and follow me either, which I was thankful for. I came in, took a long shower to get the blood off my arms, and that was it. Sleep came easy after that.

I immediately called Sam before climbing out of my bed, eager to make sure she was okay. If we had been at the bar alone, just the two of us, I never would've left her, not under even the worst of circumstances. But since she was with Luke, I figured she would at least make it home safely.

"Hey, what happened to you guys last night?" she answered, sounding way too happy for my somber mood.

"You really don't know?" I asked wearily.

"No. Syd, are you okay?" her concerned voice replied. I heard a male voice in the background, and I could hear her whisper something about giving her a minute.

"Are you with Luke?" I questioned.

"Yeah," she said happily. "When we realized you ditched us, we had to get a ride from one of his friends. I assumed that was your way of encouraging me to stay with him," she explained with slight giggle. "I'm still at his place. What's up?"

I choked back the tears, hoping not to shed a single one about this today. "I just, well, I want to talk," I said hesitantly, not even sure where to begin. "What are you doing later?"

"Hanging with you," she said warmly. She was truly the best kind of friend. "What time? Do you want to catch a volleyball game at the beach or just go somewhere to chat?"

"Yeah, later," I agreed, wanting to give her plenty of time to enjoy her morning. My problems could wait. After all, I guess I really didn't *have* a problem anymore. Cole dropped me off and left, so maybe that would be the end of it. I think he finally realized how mad I was.

We made vague plans to hang out sometime that afternoon for a little beach time and some grub. She was going to call me later whenever she parted from Luke. We worked together at the clinic tomorrow, so I knew we would have plenty of time to talk about it then, but a beach day and some food with my best friend after the traumatizing night I had, it was so needed. I wondered if she would even be able to sympathize with me though considering how love-struck she sounded.

I didn't plan to have a productive morning at all. I stretched, worked on some commands with Dexter, trying to ignore the fact that it was my last day with him, and made some eggs for a late breakfast. Finally around ten I decided to head out for a walk to clear my head.

I threw on some shorts and a tank top and opened my front door. My heart stopped as I realized there was someone sitting on my steps, leaning up against my house. He appeared to be sleeping.

"Cole?" I questioned, causing him to stir. "What are you doing?"

"I told you I wouldn't leave you," he replied directly, trying to stand up. He was still wearing his clothes from the night before and his hands and arms were still caked in blood.

"You're a mess. Why didn't you go home?"

"Because I've never said anything to you that I didn't mean," he said candidly, wincing in pain as his muscles moved. "I know you were pissed at me last night, and now that I've had twelve hours to think about it, I'm understanding it a little better."

I didn't want to smile at him, I swear. But his words were so sincere that I couldn't help it. And the fact that he spent the entire night and half the morning on my steps as he was, I knew that meant something. He was really trying.

"Cole, I just..." I hesitated, unsure of what to say. I didn't rehearse this conversation beforehand, because honestly, I wasn't sure I would even be speaking to him again.

"I know I'm not good enough for you, Syd. I've known that from the moment I saw you. But you make me want to try *so* hard to be that for you."

I stared at him as he spoke, and my heart hurt. I believed his words. I really did. Not because the way he said them, or how he phrased them. But the look in his eyes as he said it, that mattered. He had to be the only man in the world who could look so gentle and honest while covered in someone else's blood. I wanted to be mad at him. I was so fearful of him just hours earlier, but the way he looked at me – there was nothing to fear in his expression.

"You told me last night that I hurt you," he continued. "That crushed me." His eyes looked so sincere. "Please don't give up on me."

"I don't know how to do this," I said truthfully, trying to hold back some emotion in my voice. "Everything that happened last night, it was terrifying. I didn't even recognize you." Despite my best efforts, a slow tear fell down my cheek. "You really scared me last night."

"Syd, please don't cry. I hate this. I never want to be the reason you feel like this."

"Me either," I said quietly. I didn't mean it to be hurtful, I was just being honest.

"There's so much I want to tell you," he replied with such sincerity. "I'm not making any excuses for what I did, I know it was horrible. But there's so much more to the story. You have to trust that you are safe with me. I would never hurt you. You are as safe as you'll possibly ever be with me. I would never let anything bad happen to you. I'm sorry you were scared, I really am. But you have to know I will stop at nothing to protect you. You have nothing to be scared of."

"Cole, I don't see violence the same way as you do. That was really awful under any circumstances. The way you lost control like that – you were hitting him and he wasn't even moving."

"I know," he replied somberly. I could hear the regret in his voice. "When I get like that, it's like I'm outside of my own body. It's like I can't control what's happening."

"*When* you get like that? How often does this happen? How are you not in jail?"

"I've been in jail before," he said hesitantly. "I'm not going to tell you this is the first fight I've ever been in. But there's so much more to tell you."

I stared at him, feeling so conflicted. I wasn't sure why we were even having this conversation. I'd meant what I said last night about not wanting to know any more about him.

This was all so far away from my comfort level. But the way he stood here in front of me, looking so disheveled and defeated – I couldn't help but want to fix him. I so badly wanted to turn him back into the guy I saw on the boat yesterday; the guy I ate tacos with and watched baby turtles with. *That* Cole – that was a guy I was so easily falling for before last night. I hated how quickly things had changed.

"That was the same guy who stabbed me the night I met you," he began, filling the silence whether I wanted to hear it or not. "I had no intentions of retaliating for that. Honestly, before I met you, I would've had something done to that guy within twenty-four hours of it happening. But in some strange, sick deranged way, I was thankful for it. Because that's what brought me to you."

The sentiment in his voice was sweet, despite the odd circumstances.

"I left it alone. I genuinely for the first time ever didn't care about it. You made me feel like I had more important things to do with my time." He smiled at me as he said it and I couldn't help but smile back at him.

"The way he talked to you and looked at you, I just… snapped. I hated the way that part of my life was overlapping with the goodness I found in you," he said sincerely. "I felt those two worlds colliding and I just wanted it to be over. And then I reacted, which you witnessed, unfortunately."

"Do you at all feel like maybe we just shouldn't be together?" I asked softly. I felt like it was a rhetorical question, even though for so many reasons I wanted him to change my mind.

"Nothing could make me feel that way," he answered, shaking his head. "I promise you, I will do whatever it takes to make this right. To do right by you. To be better for you."

"Cole," I sighed, accepting he was not making this easy on me. "You're covered in blood. Your face is still swollen. I don't even know what to do about you."

"So help me clean up?" he suggested with a mischievous smile.

"That is so disturbing," I said dramatically, rolling my eyes.

"Look, I'm not promising you I'm the perfect guy, Syd. I know I have some flaws. I know I'm broken. But I'm working on it. You give me so much reason to work on it." He leaned in and gently brushed his lips against mine.

"Will you make me a promise?" I asked as he slowly pulled away.

"Anything."

"Will you never kiss me again while wearing someone else's blood all over your shirt?" I snickered.

"I will promise you that," he said with a slight laugh, moving us both inside my condo. "And I hear you loud and clear." In one swift motion he removed his shirt, and I remembered all over again one of the many reasons I fell so quickly for him.

"I'm serious, go take a shower before this goes any further," I stated, pointing him towards the stairs.

"You realize these swollen hands of mine are never going to get me close enough to your clean standards," he mused. "I'm going to need some help."

"There are so many things wrong with what's happening right now," I said with animated arms, following him up the stairs. "I feel like an accomplice."

"You are," he teased, kissing me one more time before we headed into the bathroom. "Which means now you're stuck with me. You know too much."

CHAPTER 13

"So I really get to stay at your place tonight?" I asked as we headed towards West Cove in his truck. Apparently Cole's shower knocked some sense into him. He was finally so much more open to letting me into his world. Sam was still busy with Luke when I texted her so we canceled our beach idea. That meant I technically didn't have any plans. That probably helped tip the scales in his favor. He promised me tacos and a night at his place. It seemed so simple, but that's what I loved about him. He was simple. And that was enough for me.

"Yes," he said reluctantly, "but I swear, it's not impressive. At all. I just want to make sure you have extremely low expectations."

"I don't care what it looks like," I said honestly. It really didn't matter to me at all. I just wanted him to make sense to me. Knowing more about his past, that helped. I imaged knowing more about his current situation would help as well. When we were together, it was amazing. He treated me so well when it was just the two of us. He was funny and caring and I could see the way he felt in his eyes – that was so comforting to me, because I felt like I never had to guess what was going on in his brain when we were together. But the rest of it, our differences – I was so worried those would tear us apart, and I genuinely wanted to overcome that.

We stopped by Antonio's on the way to Cole's place and we got our food to go. Cole remembered the exact tacos I loved from our date and he ordered the same kind, remembering which ones were too spicy for me. He was very thoughtful like that. Once we had our food we continued the drive further into West Cove.

We finally pulled up a dirt road, heading towards the trees. It looked similar to the road we were on last night after the bar. It was far more secluded than all of the roads closer to the lake, filled with streetlights and tourists. This was a totally different world.

There were some trailers here and there with dirty old mailboxes out front. Some had boards over their windows where the glass had been shattered, and it looked quite depressing. There were old plastic toys scattered out front of most of the properties, leading me to believe there were full families living in some of the dilapidated structures. I'd never seen anything like this back home in Chicago.

Cole pulled up a small driveway that led to a beautiful, good-sized log cabin. It looked far more majestic than all of the other living spaces we saw on the way. Behind that cabin I could see five or six other cabins, much smaller in size. It almost looked like a campground of sorts. There looked to be some communal spaces, but each cabin also had its own little area for parking and such. Towards the very back of the property, I could see a large building of some sort. I imagined that was the 'warehouse' Cole referred to occasionally.

"So, the main house is Harvey's of course," Cole explained, pointing to the log cabin. "He lives there with his wife Sonita."

"He's married?" I asked with a surprised tone. I guess I'd never really asked, but it just struck me as odd the way Cole talked about him. He almost made it sound like it was just the two of them all the time. I didn't realize there was a woman.

"Yeah, over forty years," he replied with a smirk. "I know you've heard some unfavorable things about him, about his line of work and everything. But deep down he's a good guy. He loves Sonita like I've never seen in anyone else."

I smiled as he said it. I guess he *did* have a good role model in Harvey on some levels. "That's beautiful," I stated wistfully.

"He's taught me a lot. He's always stressed three things to me. Stand up for yourself, work hard, and do right by the one who loves you." He stared at me with his intense eyes. I treasured these moments with him when he spoke with such seriousness. "He's lived that way his whole life. I guess that's why I look up to him so much. All those things have mattered to me."

"Is that why you do everything you do for him?" I asked quietly as he pulled into a small lot next to one of the undersized cabins behind Harvey's.

"He's the only one I know to do right by," he shrugged. "No one has ever cared for me the way Harvey has. I was such a shattered, tormented little boy. I thought the entire world gave up on me. Then he came along and proved to me that I hadn't been completely given up on after all. He was the first and only person who remained present in my life. I owe him a lot for that."

I completely understood what he was saying. I truly did, given the life he'd had. But I also wondered how far that loyalty went. I wondered what kinds of things Harvey expected from him. I wondered if Harvey took advantage of Cole in that way, knowing he felt that kind of obligation towards him. I wondered how much of the trouble Cole got in – whether that was his own doing, or Harvey's.

"So this is paradise," he said, interrupting my stream of thoughts. He stretched his arms out to a cute little cabin complete with a screen door and window boxes. There were no flowers in them of course, but they screamed with potential. The place was far cuter than I expected it to be. "Oh no, don't do that. You're already building it up," he said, wagging a finger near my face. "I see that look in your eyes, like when you see an animal – you think it's adorable and you get really excited.

But this place is *not* adorable. You're going to want a tetanus shot before you leave."

"Come on, take me inside," I said with a laugh. He shut off the truck and we climbed out. The trees surrounding us looked majestic. The property itself wasn't necessarily awe-inspiring, but it offered so much – space to run, some privacy, and even a concrete basketball court towards the back.

"This used to be a campground a long time ago," he explained, leading me towards the front door. "Harvey acquired it about twenty years ago. Right now only a few of the other cabins have residents – those people tend to come and go. I've lived in this one here ever since I was a teenager." He opened the door and it was dimly lit. I was surprised to find it was essentially just a rectangular box inside. "It looks like a charming log cabin, right? But it's actually just a modular box structure they attached logs to on the outside. Tourists used to come here to camp and they sold it to them as these little log cabin bungalows. I've always wondered how many people realized that's not exactly the case."

There was a small kitchen area, a queen sized bed in one corner, a bistro table, and a door on the opposite end which I assumed was a bathroom. He kept everything organized, but he was right – it wasn't exactly adorable. The old linoleum floor was peeled up along the corners and seams and the laminate countertops were scraped and chipped. It was definitely from another time period.

"This isn't terrible," I said honestly. I mean it was livable. I certainly would've made more of an effort to spruce the place up a bit, but for a guy, it could be far worse.

"That's the nicest thing anyone's ever said about this place," he teased. "Come on. We're eating outside."

He grabbed some blankets from underneath his bed and led me back to his truck where he opened up the tailgate. He spread out the blankets and lifted me up into the back of the truck with such ease.

"Out here in the woods this is what we call fine dining," he said sarcastically. "Tacos, a stereo, and stars – that's all we need."

"This is perfect," I said sincerely as he spread out our food. The sun had set and the stars overhead began to light up the sky. The air was perfectly calm and it was actually quite pleasant out.

"So this is it. The night of truths, right?" he mused, handing me my food. "I think you promised to tell me all of your dark, dirty secrets or something."

I shot him a playful look. "So far *you* are my darkest secret," I teased. "I've never dated a guy with a record. Or tattoos. Or a 1950s linoleum floor."

He laughed at me. "Really? So you're saying I'm the worst thing you've ever done?"

"I wouldn't word it like that," I stated with a slight laugh, trying to keep the mood light. "But from your point of view, I think it's fair to say that my life experiences have been pretty sheltered up until now."

"Well I'm glad I can help you live a little," he teased back. He smiled at me and I was so happy we were here together. If he hadn't stayed outside my condo all night, I wondered how this would've played out. Would I have given in and called him anyway? I wasn't sure. But either way I was so glad he didn't have a single bit of hesitation when it came to us. "You probably want to start asking me questions, right?" he said with a smirk. "I know that's what you've been waiting for. This is it. I won't hold anything back."

"Maybe you should start from the beginning," I shrugged, unsure of what to even ask. There was so much to know.

"Well you know how I ended up with Harvey," he began, leaning back on his elbows. "Once my father went to jail, his sister took off from the trailer we were staying in down the road. So I was literally left all alone. Once Harvey took me in, I obviously grew up watching what he did. He always had all of these things going on. The bike shop, he actually owns it. It's just a little further up the road that way," he said pointing. "It's partly a chop shop though, so although that's the most innocent place I work for a living, it still comes with some problems. I mean don't get me wrong, I don't do anything illegal there myself, per se. I just work on the bikes. But I'm not totally oblivious to the fact that some of the parts I use are stolen."

He looked up at me, waiting for my judgment. I honestly didn't have any at the moment, I wanted to hear so much more.

"Harvey has all of these other circuits," he continued, trying to break it down for me. "He's got some kind of gambling ring going on, that's been in place for years. I think my dad used to be involved in that in some way. A lot of the wrong people owe Harvey money, and sometimes collecting that money gets messy. Like I told you before, my job is essentially to just pick up money and deliver it back to him. Sometimes he has people to pay himself and I make those drops for him also. But sometimes those exchanges don't go well."

"And that's why you were stabbed outside of my clinic, right?" I asked softly. "Over money?"

"Yes, with a little blackmail thrown in," he answered honestly. "Someone has some dirt on him, but I don't know what that is, or if it's even valid. Harvey rarely ever does a drop himself, but that night he insisted on doing it for some reason. That's how I knew it wasn't just about money, there had to be something else going on. I told him

I could deliver the package myself, but he refused to let me. I followed him that night, obviously for good reason. Harvey always taught me to trust my instincts, and the whole thing just didn't feel right. The fact that he wanted to do the deal alone, that was a red flag. Anyway, he got stabbed and I tried to intervene. I hit the guy pretty hard and got him off Harvey, but his knife still got my arm. Then, ironically, a light turned on in your clinic."

I thought back to that night. Was that when Eva went into the supply room to get the net for her dead fish? There was a window in there.

"I think it spooked the guy, like someone heard what was going on. He saw the light and panicked. He told me that wasn't the end of things and he would find me, and then he took off."

What a random thing to happen with the light from the clinic. It was scary to think about what would've happened if the light was never flipped on. I was suddenly so thankful for Eva's inept fish care. I watched Cole as he spoke, so relieved that he was finally letting it all out. I didn't want any more secrets or omissions.

"I saw how bad Harvey was bleeding, and at first he refused to let me help him, but I had to. The nearest building was yours." He smiled as he said it. "The second I saw you, I…" He paused, trying to think of how to say what he wanted. "It's like I forgot for a moment what had just happened. You were there in your scrubs with your blonde hair tied up and all I could think was that you looked so far away from where I was. Not your physical distance, but I mean *you.* You looked so professional and put together and you were in a vet office, doing something *good* – and here I was, interrupting you with violence."

"The blood freaked me out initially, but you looked eerily calm for the situation," I recalled.

"Probably because I was mesmerized by you," he smirked. "I was trying to act cool and nonchalant, like it was no big deal. But honestly I was completely panicked. I knew Harvey was in some kind of deep trouble at that point. Not from his wound, but by the whole situation. Harvey never lets his guard down like that, so I knew something was very wrong."

"How much do you really know about what Harvey does?" I questioned.

"Honestly, more than I should, but not nearly enough," he tried to explain. "I know there are drugs going in and out of his warehouse. I don't have anything to do with that either, but I guarantee you the money I'm touching is directly related to that. Harvey tries to keep me out of the loop on a lot of it so that if the operation gets busted, I'll be in the clear. I doubt I'm so clear though."

"So why do you do it?" I asked sincerely. He sounded like he had at least some small amount of conviction about it, knowing it was wrong.

"I can't turn my back on the only person who never turned their back on me," he said with such an honest voice. "I think about it all the time. It weighs on me, heavily. I've seen things I don't want to see, and I've done things I don't want to do. But he's done more for me than anyone else in my life. I don't know how to walk away from that."

His loyalty to Harvey astounded me. I wasn't sure I could do it. But at the same time, I hadn't lived his life. No one had ever given up on me. I couldn't imagine the bond they shared over that.

"I think it's more my doing than Harvey," he confessed. "Growing up, by the time I was a teenager, I saw the kind of money he brought in. I knew that was the only thing that would ever get me out of this town. I begged him incessantly to let me in on it. He refused for awhile. I swear he genuinely didn't want me involved in any of it. He kept telling me he wanted something more for me. Imagine that."

I crossed my legs in front of me and stared at him. Moments like this with Cole, when he was completely honest about his life – they felt so intimate and unspoiled. His words were heartbreaking, and I wished he had such a different story. But knowing how he became this person he was, it mattered so much to me. Beyond that, knowing how hard he was working to change his situation, that was the most inspiring part. He genuinely sounded like he wanted something different.

"By the time I was eighteen or nineteen though, Harvey finally let me help him out with a few things," he continued. "It was nothing big, just a few errands for him. But people started making comments about me, about my size. Like I was a threat to them if they didn't do what Harvey wanted. I think that was the turning point for him. He realized he could use me, even just for intimidation, and that would help him out and he could give me a cut of the money which benefited me. It just got deeper from there."

"Have you ever told him no? To anything he's asked of you?" I wondered how far his loyalty and obligation went.

"Only once," he replied hesitantly. He shook his head like he didn't want to continue, but he didn't hold back. "A couple years back, my dad was released from jail. He was barely out a week before he was busted for a burglary. Harvey asked me to take the heat for him. My dad has a pretty extensive record, he's been in and out of prison since before I was born. Harvey knew if he took the fall for it, they would lock him up for awhile, versus if it was me, I would probably only get a few months sentence. He told me that if my dad went away for long, it would impact the 'business' and he couldn't afford that, since my dad had some ties to people he knew. Whatever that meant. So he wanted me to confess to the crime."

"You look up to him like a father, and he asked you to go to prison for someone else?" I said astounded. He asked him to do it for his deadbeat biological father no less. Most things he said about Harvey before seemed so much more admirable. Obviously his business deals were one thing, but they way he took Cole in, I couldn't imagine that conversation. How could he ask that of him?

"I understood where he was coming from," he said with a shrug. "On paper it made sense. And honestly, if it was for anybody else I would've strongly considered it, especially if it meant a lot to Harvey. But not for my father. I couldn't do it."

I could hear the emotion in his voice. It was sad and angry at the same time. "So that's what your dad has been in jail for the past couple of years?"

"Yeah, he was sentenced for four."

"Have you talked to him since he's been in jail?" I asked quietly.

"Once, but we only exchanged a few words." Cole fell quiet and I looked up at the treetops above us, blocking some of the stars. It felt like such a private spot, like we were in the middle of nowhere. It seemed like a perfect spot to share these kinds of stories. I appreciated his honestly probably more than he realized, but I definitely wanted him to lead the conversation. "I was in twice. Just briefly."

"You went in to see him?"

"No," he replied, growing quieter. "That's when I was *in* jail. I saw him as an inmate."

I was shocked, and had no idea what to say. I was not expecting that admission. He'd mentioned having some run-ins with the law, but for some reason I assumed that was long ago, maybe even back when he was a teenager. No wonder he didn't say much when we first met. Honestly that would've made me run.

"Say something," he said softly.

"I… you… why?" I stammered, not sure what to ask.

"I was picked up for dumb stuff," he admitted. "Wrong place wrong time, that kind of thing. I was only held both times for a couple nights. Harvey paid my bonds and that was it. The cops weren't after me, they just wanted information."

"How long ago was that?" I wondered. When he originally mentioned jail time, I hoped for some story about how that was years ago and he'd changed his ways since, but clearly it had to be in the last couple years.

"One was about a year ago. I saw my father that time, but we didn't speak. I wasn't sure he even knew I was there. The other time was maybe four months ago?" he estimated.

"Cole," I said quietly, not sure what I even wanted to say. He reached out his arms to me and pulled me in. "You were in jail just four months ago?"

"Now do you understand why I've been putting off this conversation?" he asked sincerely. "I know it's bad. And inexcusable. I'm not making excuses for it either, I can say all day long that it's Harvey, getting me mixed up in all this. But at the end of the day, I know I have a choice. But I just… I can't get out."

"Do you even want to?" I pulled back and looked at his eyes, trying to gauge his emotion.

"I always said I did. I wanted to, but maybe not bad enough. And then I saw you at the clinic, and I'm telling you, something changed for me. You had this innocence about you. You're more compassionate without reason than anyone I've ever known. You fix things, right? Animals, people… And I don't know, I just… I want to be fixed."

"I can't fix myself, so I don't know what to do with you," I said lightheartedly.

"You could at least tell me your prison stories to make me feel better about myself?" he replied sarcastically.

"So what's your plan?" I asked, not sure what to even do with all of this information.

"Honestly, my plan all along, even before you, was to do one last big job for Harvey, for the money, and then head out," he explained. "Down the coast. Far away from all this. But now, here with you, I can't imagine going anywhere. I feel so conflicted… About everything. But I know I have to make a change."

I wasn't sure how to respond. It was as if he was looking to me for an answer, but I couldn't have been farther away in relating to his situation.

"If you could have everything you want, would you leave this place?" he asked seriously.

"I don't even know what I want," I replied honestly. "I have nothing keeping me here anymore. School's over, and even Sam is leaving next month, which I'm in denial about. But…"

"What do you mean you don't know what you want? I thought you wanted to run your own animal rescue sanctuary?" he asked, cutting me off.

"Well I mean sure, that's just a dream. Like an 'off in the distant future' dream. I'd also like 300 pairs of shoes and a boat and a pasta maker. But you can't just *want* things. That's not enough. Even a spoiled city girl like me knows that. No one gets everything they want."

"How do you know?" he asked with genuine eyes. "What if it's possible?"

"Are you telling me *you* believe that?" I asked with an amused grin. This entire conversation felt backwards. *I* was supposed to be the delusional naïve one.

"I never did before," he replied. "My whole life suggests that's an impossibility. But for a girl like you to give me a chance… If that's possible? Then yeah, everything else seems easier than that."

"What are you saying?" I narrowed my eyes at him.

"I don't know, I just…" he paused, gathering his thoughts. "I just want to know that I can be enough for you. I mean, I know you can't answer that right now. But I want to know what the right thing is to do. I can't be good enough for you if I stay here. I know that. But I won't leave here without you."

On the surface those words seemed like a boyish ideal – the whole "I'll never leave without you" thing. It was dramatic, and let's face it, usually not true. But I thought back to last night, when he promised me he wasn't going anywhere – and sure enough, his words were completely literal. He didn't leave my steps. I believed him in that moment that if I was still in the picture, he wouldn't make it to California like he'd always planned.

"What are you thinking?" he asked softly.

"I don't know," I replied honestly. "Like maybe I'm holding you back?"

He laughed quietly, shaking his head. "You think *you're* holding me back?" He continued laughing. "All I want is to be a better person for you. That's what I want. But honestly I don't know how to do it. It all weighs on me, like I just need *one* more big job. That's it. Then I would have enough."

"Have enough? What does that even mean? What's enough?"

He got up and jumped off the back of the tailgate, heading inside his cabin. He reemerged with a small metal box, climbing back into the truck. He opened the box and handed me a business card and a couple brochures.

"What are these?" I asked, browsing through them. They looked like plots of land for sale.

"That's what I'm trying to do. That's the land I want to buy in California. It's ten acres."

I studied the pictures. It was a beautiful open lot surrounded by a dirt road and trees everywhere. *Avocado trees.* I smirked as I realized it. The business card was for the realtor selling the property.

"This is where you're going?" I asked, looking at his face. He looked so happy as he talked about it.

"I hope so," he sighed. "But I'm not there yet." He held up a huge roll of money. "I still need like, forty grand or so."

"Cole, what are you doing with all that money," I said with a panicked tone. It was way too much to keep in a metal box somewhere in his house. "Have you heard of those places called banks? They handle that kind of thing for you," I said sarcastically.

"This isn't the full one-sixty," he responded with a laugh.

"One sixty?" I repeated, clearly confused.

"Yeah, I have a hundred and sixty thousand dollars saved up so far," he shrugged. "But I need at least two hundred thousand in cash to make the purchase before a bank will let me finance the rest."

"You have a hundred and sixty thousand dollars just lying around your house? You can't keep that kind of money tucked under your bed," I urged. "You really are a crazy person."

"It's not all here," he smirked. "I keep it hidden in multiple places."

"Cole, seriously, you need a bank!" I repeated, wondering how on earth he thought storing large amounts of money in a dingy cabin was a good idea.

"I can't hand it over to a bank, they need a paper trail for that kind of money," he explained. "I would be flagged immediately. I told you, it's not necessarily from an upstanding source. The last thing I need is people checking into what I do. It's not like this comes with tax forms."

"So you've been in jail, you've been violently stabbed and beaten on numerous occasions, you work in a chop shop, you handle drug money, *and* you're committing tax fraud?" I said audibly.

"Of all those things you're really getting hung up on the taxes?" he teased. "Come on, Syd, I told you, I'm not perfect. But I'm trying to change. I swear."

"I'm pretty sure you're on some type of FBI Most Wanted List," I replied, only half sarcastically. "Cole, all of that is *really* bad." I was trying to process it all in my head, but I just couldn't. He wasn't necessarily justifying any of it, he also knew it was wrong. And I believed that maybe, *just maybe,* he wanted to change. But he seemed so far away from my life at the moment. He was more like one of the Dateline episodes my dad always watched. But yet here I was, looking at him with stupid googly eyes just because he had a perfect handsome face and giant biceps. He was like quicksand.

"Why are you so quiet? Say something," he said softly.

"Honestly all of this makes me worry about you," I admitted. "I love spending time with you, I really do. You make me laugh and smile incessantly and I think about you every moment we're not together." I knew I shouldn't be telling him all of this, but it was just pouring out of my mouth. The honesty in his eyes brought out every truth I felt inside of myself. "I love everything about *this,*" I continued, holding my hands up. Tacos and stargazing in the back of his truck – it was a perfect summer night on so many levels. I wanted to end up wrapped in his arms by the end of the evening feeling cared for and safe, with no regard for anything else happening around us. I hated all of these things hanging over my head – all of the things he was admitting to me just to save whatever this was. I appreciated his honesty, I really did. But it also genuinely scared me. "I just… I mean, what if you go to jail again? Cole, I am not the girl who can handle this kind of thing. I'm not."

"Because you are *good*," he said softly. "I know I don't deserve your goodness. But that's all I want, to be the guy who deserves a girl like you. I promise I'm getting out of all this and it will all be behind me. All of it. I just need a little more time."

"Don't you feel like you've been saying that for awhile?" I shrugged. I couldn't imagine I was the only reason he wanted to change.

"Yeah," he answered reluctantly. "But despite wanting something else, I just never had a good enough reason to stop, and it kept pulling me back in." He gently touched my face. "I don't deserve your trust just because I'm asking for it, but I'm begging for it anyway. I actually called Harvey last night while I was sitting in your doorway. That was finally it for me. I told him I needed out."

"I don't know exactly what you mean by that," I replied quietly. "You quit?"

"I told him I'm laying low right now. I'm not making drops for him and I'm not doing anything around the warehouse anymore," he began. "He actually took it well. Better than I thought anyway, but I think he knew the time was coming. Honestly he didn't even try to talk me out of it. I told him what happened at the bar. I reminded him my whole life that he told me I had to do right by the one who cares about me. All I could think about in that moment was how that person was you."

"And that's it? He'll just let you go?" I asked for clarification.

"Yeah, for the most part. As of now, I have no more responsibilities to Harvey. I have nothing on the side, nothing I'm out doing for him, I have no business with him. I'll work a little at the bike shop, but that's it. I should probably pay him some rent now that I'm not earning my keep in other ways. But other than that, I'll have no other responsibilities other than being good to you." He looked at me with such a genuine sweet expression, I swear my entire body tingled. "No violence. No dangerous errands for Harvey. The bike shop will just be to pass the time while you're at the vet clinic saving the world." His lips curled up into a sweet smile. "And then I'll ravage and adore you every second after that when you're free to spend time with me. And we can figure all of this out."

"Assuming I want to spend my spare time with you," I said coyly, not wanting to show him how much I truly wanted that.

"I'm hoping I can talk you into that," he said with a sexy grin, pulling my face close to his. "Let me convince you why you should." He kissed me eagerly and I melted into him. Despite everything he had just told me, all of the horrible things he was a part of, I couldn't help but submit to him. He made me feel so many things, and not one of them was remorse for choosing to be with him despite his flaws.

He held me tight and I clung back to him. Every touch of his was sweet and tender, yet commanding all at the same time, like he knew exactly what to do with me. I knew in this moment, under the perfect starlit sky, that *this* was what I wanted. Cole was my choice, no matter the path he was on. I knew this was the beginning of *us* – our paths colliding and becoming the same.

I couldn't imagine a moment when I would ever regret falling for him. Even if such a time came – I was certain the crash would be worth it.

CHAPTER 14

The next morning we awoke completely wrapped up in each other exactly like I'd hoped. The blankets were tangled tightly around us and we were still in the back of his truck, watching the sun come up. In these simple, beautiful moments with him, there was no right or wrong – no good or bad – it was just simply *us*. And that felt like enough. In so many ways, I wanted time to stop – I wanted each second with him to draw out until the rest of the world didn't exist. But instead, time passed like the breeze that whispered through the trees in these woods surrounding the lake.

I had to work all day, that was inevitable. But as soon as I got off work, I couldn't wait to rush into his arms at the end of my day.

"I've completely changed my mind," I said to him as we grabbed some dinner at a local spot near the clinic.

At first his face looked worried, but then it softened. "Please tell me this isn't bad," he said nervously.

"I want you to take me for a ride on your motorcycle," I replied with a smile.

"Seriously?" he snickered. "Really?"

"Yes. I want to know what it feels like."

"I thought this day would never come," he said excitedly. "Tonight?"

I nodded, happy he was so eager to take me. I'd never been into motorcycles. They seemed so dangerous and unsafe. But the more I thought about Cole, he was those things too in many ways. Yet I completely trusted him. I wanted to experience something he loved, even though it terrified me.

After we ate, we headed back to his place to get his bike. He explained a few things to me, like why it was important to wear my sunglasses while we were riding, along with how to lean my body into the turns. We climbed on it and he started up the motorcycle. I wrapped my arms around him as tightly as possible, and we headed out. It was so much more than I was expecting.

The wind rushed around our bodies, and it felt like we were flying in some weird way. It was a completely different sense of freedom than anything I'd ever felt before. The trees breezed past us and the lake sparkled as we hugged the curves of the road. Any fear I had of doing something new, I knew as long as Cole was with me, any nerves I had would dissipate. He felt so firm and strong and safe underneath my tight grip, and I felt he would always feel that way to me – as if he was completely unbreakable. Any reservations I had about him when we met – they were completely gone now, left in the wind behind us. I knew this was everything I had ever wanted.

This day became our new routine – we spent all of our spare time together, trying new things, exploring the area around us - but also returning to the uncomplicated joy of simply just being with each other. One day blended into the next, and I felt as though I would never stop radiating with the happiness I felt from our time spent together.

Over the passing weeks, we fell in love the way every girl imagines at least once in her lifetime. We splashed each other under the summer sun, and we spent long, warm nights beneath thin linen sheets. We jumped off rocks into crystal blue water, and laid out in the bed of his truck under so many starlit skies. The world above us became our ceiling as we talked beside late night fires and woke up to so many glimmers of light peeking over the mountaintops with each sunrise. We played and we laughed and we dreamed about the world like it had no end in mind for us. It was strange in some ways how a girl from the city and a boy from the woods could carry on the way we did. But I feared nothing with his protection, and he dreamed beyond the treetops he stared at every night when he was a child.

Before him, I'd felt cared for. I'd felt lust and adoration and so many other things. But this love was so different – it was fierce and intense and all-consuming. It was passionate and deep and intimate and it left no room for pause or hesitation. That was the part that hit me the hardest. Before Cole, I second guessed everything. Honestly, even when I met him, I still did. I never felt sure enough about any decision I'd ever made. My heart ached when my mom passed and I held so much guilt when I tried to live life afterwards, like I didn't deserve to move forward. I dwelled on my college major, torn between disappointing my father or myself. I hesitated when Ian wanted to move us towards a busy life I never dreamed of. But with Cole, there was no pause – no doubt that my dreams could in fact be the same as his.

We didn't really talk about California. With Harvey somewhat out of the picture, at least not involved in Cole's day-to-day routine, it almost didn't matter. We didn't have to discuss "someday" because every passing day started and ended with us together – and that was more than we needed. But one night, lying in the sand around a bonfire with Sam and Luke, spending her last night in Mountain Ridge together before she headed to Oregon, so many things changed.

"I can't believe this is it," I said for the millionth time as I squeezed her hand. The boys were throwing things into the fire, amused each time the flames grew higher. My eyes filled with tears and I so badly wanted to keep them back, but I knew I would fail.

"I would be so much more devastated about this if I was leaving you alone," she said with a full heart. "But look at you, you are so deliriously happy. Just like you used to be before you started taking on everyone else's guilt."

"I can't believe that doesn't weigh on my mind every single day like it used to," I said quietly. Honestly there were so many days that passed where I didn't think about Ian or the accident at all. It would never be completely removed from my mind, I knew that. Nor did I ever want to forget it. Ian loved me right, and I knew I was better off for that. His memory didn't deserve to be erased. I wondered sometimes if I was able to love Cole better because of what I'd learned from that relationship. But to finally feel like I could breathe again without it weighing so heavily on my chest, I felt so free.

"You will forever be my best friend," Sam said with tears rolling down her eyes. "I know we said we wouldn't fall apart, but there's no way around this."

Tears fell from my eyes as well, and we hugged so tight. In reality she was only going to be a nine hour drive away, or about an hour flight. It could've been more drastic, I knew that. But not seeing her at the clinic several days a week, and missing out on our beach afternoons, those were going to kill me. But she was right. This was so much easier to do now that I wasn't on my own. I smiled at Cole through the firelight, fighting my tears, and he simply winked at me and smiled, as if to reassure me the world would still be okay.

Sam and Luke, as casual as they tried to keep it, didn't look so casual as we said our goodbyes. She wanted to spend one last night with him, and I completely understood. We hugged again for at least five lingering minutes, and kissed each other's cheeks one last time as we finally parted ways. She promised to call me as soon as she made it to Oregon tomorrow afternoon, and despite my tears and swollen eyes, I was so very happy for her. She was accomplishing everything she ever wanted, and I couldn't have wished for anything else for her.

Cole wrapped a tight arm around my shoulders as we made our way back to his truck. His skin on mine lifted my mood, and I looked forward to the way he would hold me tonight whether I was an emotional mess or not. It didn't matter to him. He loved me the same through all of my moods and I couldn't have been more grateful for that.

As we climbed in his truck, his phone rang. His happy expression turned sour instantly as he read the name on the screen.

"Hello?" he said with some confusion. There was a long pause. The voice on the other end was too quiet for me to hear, but I gathered by Cole's face that it wasn't a welcome conversation. He let out a few 'yeahs' and 'okays' but that was it. When he finally hung up, he started up the truck and turned out of the beach lot towards my condo.

"Is everything okay?" I asked sincerely.

"No," he said quietly. "That was Harvey." He didn't offer any more.

“Is he doing okay?” I replied with concern. Surely Cole had more to say about the call. He looked like he saw a ghost, but it was just a quick conversation.

“He’s fine,” Cole replied dismissively. “I know this is horrible timing. I know Sam leaving is hard on you. But I have to go somewhere tonight,” he said vaguely.

“Why are you seeing Harvey?” I questioned. As far as I knew, he really hadn’t dealt with him much since he told him he was done working for him. I was always a little skeptical about it, I couldn’t help it. They had such a strong bond, so it made sense that I would wonder from time to time if Harvey had any plans to pull Cole back into whatever he was up to. The unsettling pit in my stomach told me that was exactly what was happening. “Cole, please talk to me.”

“Syd,” he sighed, pulling the truck over on the side of the road. He ran his fingers through his hair and I could tell he was frustrated.

“No secrets, Cole. That’s how this works.”

“I know,” he said softly. “But I just don’t want to worry you unnecessarily. It’s probably nothing.”

“The look on your face doesn’t suggest it’s nothing,” I replied. “What’s going on?” I hated in that moment that I felt like we were back at the beginning – back when he was scared to tell me his secrets. Rightfully so, I didn’t understand them at the time. I was still baffled by how a guy like him, as sweet and honest as anyone I'd ever known, it didn't make sense to me the way he was so dishonest in other areas of his life. But we seemed well beyond secrets. He had to know by now that nothing he could say to me would be so bad that I would change my mind about him. What I felt for him was an absolute certainty – no phone call could change that.

"Things are about to change," he answered with a stern expression. "Everything is going to change." He rested his head back on the seat and closed his eyes.

"Cole, you're scaring me," I said honestly, staring at his face. "Please tell me something."

He looked over at me and I'm sure he saw the worry in my eyes. He slid towards me and wrapped me up, pulling me into his chest. He kissed my face and stroked my hair, appearing as if he was struggling to find the right words to say to me.

"Just say it. Whatever it is," I urged.

He was silent for another minute or so, but then spoke softly.

"My dad is out of jail."

CHAPTER 15

Cole didn't tell me anything further. Instead he drove me back to my condo and walked me up to the door, kissing me as sweetly as he had so many nights before, but then he turned his back on me as he walked away towards his truck. The sound of his footsteps walking away from me felt louder than any of the other sounds around us. They echoed in my head, and my heart hurt. When Cole said things were about to change, I hoped he was just being paranoid or overly dramatic. But somehow within minutes from that admission, it became true. Everything felt different. Something pulled his attention from me and he didn't want to bring me into it – I knew that meant it was bad news. Perhaps something he couldn't fix.

I expected some type of communication from him that night – a text, or even a phone call – but none came. My restless sleep turned into an early morning, and my shift at the clinic felt infinite. I checked my phone periodically, but there was nothing new. Sam eventually sent me a message that she was alive and safe in her new home, hours and hours away from me. I wanted to feel some tinge of happiness about it, but I couldn't. I felt more alone than ever before and it ate at me.

Finally a few minutes before my shift was over, my phone rang and Cole's name appeared on the screen. I answered it quickly.

"Hello?"

"Can I come get you?" he asked eagerly.

"What's going on?"

"We need tacos," he said lightly, taking some of the tension out of the conversation. "Everything I have to tell you can only be said over Antonio's food."

"It's really that bad?" I commented.

"I told you, it's my ultimate groveling food. I need to ask for a lot of forgiveness tonight, and I can only do that over tacos."

My stomach felt uneasy and I wasn't sure I would even have an appetite. "Can you meet me at my house in about a half hour?"

He agreed and we hung up the phone. I made the short walk home and took a quick shower to revive my stale mood. I put on a cute, relatively short sundress, hoping to take his mind off whatever was bothering him. I wasn't sure a dress was enough to do that, but it was the only thing I could think of to do in that moment.

He pulled up in front of my house, right on time, and I headed out the front door as soon as I saw his truck. He wasn't even fully out of the driver's side yet before I walked up to greet him. I reached up and kissed him right on the mouth, flashing him a sexy look as I pulled away. "You have tacos and me tonight. Whatever this is, whatever is going on – we can fix it together."

He smiled back at me and wrapped his strong arms around me, lifting me up and bracing me against his truck. "Trust me, you and tacos should be enough to fix everything, I know. Just promise me you'll hear me out before you freak out." He kissed me with the kind of intensity that made me feel like no one else was around. I kissed him back hungrily, and everything felt normal, just like it had the past couple months. A car passing by honked at us loudly, and I realized it probably wasn't appropriate to have my legs wrapped around him like this while pinned up against his truck. I smiled coyly as he set me down. He opened up his door and I slid in through it to the passenger seat.

"I won't freak out," I said, still smiling at him as he fired up the truck and headed towards Antonio's. "Whatever it is, we can get through it." He was still smiling back at me and we probably looked like two idiotic love-struck teenagers, beaming in silence as we drove.

We pulled into the lot of the taco stand and climbed out of his truck. Cole ordered, just like usual, and we grabbed the food to go so we could watch the sunset from the table on the beach across the way.

He handed me my food and started talking. "So like I said, my dad is out of jail," he began, unwrapping his tacos. "Apparently he got out a lot earlier than expected – good behavior or something like that, which is a first for him. Apparently he's already gainfully employed too," he said with a heavily sarcastic tone.

"Working for Harvey?" I assumed.

"No," he replied, shaking his head. "Hence the problem. I guess he's pissed, blaming Harvey for being in jail in the first place, so he's been communicating with someone else while he's been in. One of Harvey's competitors I guess you'd say."

There was a long pause and I had so many questions, but I knew Cole needed to tell me all of this in his own way. That's how he worked best.

"Harvey needs me to do one last job," he said hesitantly.

"Cole, I thought you were done with all of that." I hated the thought of him being sucked back into that world. I always wondered if he was ever really truly going to be done with all of that.

"I know, and I am. I have been. And I will be when it's done," he explained. "But he needs me for one last thing. I have to do it."

"You *have* to? Or you want to? Or you don't have the choice to say no?" I questioned.

"Well for one, I owe Harvey this. I really do," he said convincingly. His loyalty to Harvey mattered so much, I knew that. But I'd hoped Harvey could see how far he'd come – living a normal, honest life – I wished so bad that mattered. The fact that he wanted to pull Cole back into everything he was doing, it was disheartening. I'm sure he knew Cole would give in and do it.

"I understand why you feel so loyal to Harvey," I replied. "I really do. I know he took you in and gave you a life and you feel like you wouldn't have had one otherwise. I know he did so many good things for you. But the path he had you on Cole, you have to admit that it wasn't a good one."

"I know that," he said quietly. "But this is big. And I hold a lot of responsibility in this. My dad went to jail because of me, so this whole situation is kind of my doing in the first place."

"You didn't take the fall for him, that's not the same thing," I clarified. "He's in jail because he did something wrong. You shouldn't have taken his place in that, no matter what Harvey wanted you to do."

He shook his head as I spoke, seemingly uninterested in what I was saying. "That's not really how it happened."

"Well that's the version you told me," I stated, starting to feel frustrated by this conversation.

"That's the version of the story everyone else knows," he said softly.

"What do you mean?"

"I lied about it. I was the reason he got caught in the first place." He hung his head, looking somewhat ashamed. "I left something of his at the scene." There was a long pause. "He had nothing to do with the crime. I wanted him to get in trouble."

"Why?" I asked quietly.

"Because I hated him," he replied honestly. "Because I was mad at him for the way my life turned out. I hated him for everything that had happened to me. I blamed him for the way my life was working out even up to that point. Everything that happened with Britt at the time – I blamed him for that too. Obviously a failed relationship was nothing new to me, he taught me everything I knew on that. I was never good enough for anyone, he made that clear to me my whole life. And I certainly wasn't good enough for him. He pushed that in my face every chance he got."

I wasn't sure what to say. I could tell by Cole's voice that he had so much anger and resentment towards his father. It wasn't a subject we talked about often, so I knew I didn't know the whole story. He'd left him on and off for jail, that I knew – and Cole once mentioned how cruel he was, but I was sure I had no idea of all the things Cole endured in relation to his father.

"I saw it as an opportunity. I knew it was wrong, but I just hated him so much. I had an opportunity to punish him and I took it." There was so much sadness in his voice as he spoke. I could tell he felt so much hurt towards his father. I couldn't imagine that feeling, nor could I say what I would have done in his situation. "Syd, I know

I've done so many horrible things. But you're the first *good* thing I've ever known. All I want is to get out of all this. But I feel like no matter what I do, it will always just be hanging over my head. One minute I know the right people, and then in no time they become the wrong people. I have to get out of all this, I know that. If I can just do one last thing for Harvey, that can be it. Then it will all be over."

"Won't that just make things worse?" I added objectively. "Once you're back in, won't that make everything harder? I don't understand."

"Harvey is going to pay me fifty thousand dollars for this last job," he said bluntly. "That's enough to get out."

"What do you mean? This doesn't sound like something you can buy your way out of."

"On top of what I've already saved, that will be enough to get that land in California," he shrugged. "I feel like that's the only way I can truly get out of this. I have to leave it all."

His words hit me hard. *Leave it all.* All I heard in that was that he had to leave *me.* A knot formed in my throat.

"There has to be a better way," I replied quietly.

"Come with me, Syd. Come to California with me." He stared into my eyes as he said it, and they burned through me. He looked at me with that intense stare so many times – it was always full of so much emotion. They transfixed on me like a spell, and it was so hard for me to think in those moments.

"Cole, it's too soon," I said reluctantly. "It's barely been a couple months. That's a big thing."

"I wanted to take you away from here within two minutes of meeting you," he replied with a smirk. "That night at the clinic, I saw it in you then - your compassion and good nature. And then by the time you wanted to karate chop me in your living room, that was enough. I wanted to throw you over my shoulder and strap you to my bike and just head down the coast. I would've taken you away back then. And now, after these last two months… This has been the most normal life I've ever lived, yet it feels like something more extraordinary than what anyone else gets." He reached out and touched my face, still keeping his eyes on mine. "I would never leave without you. But this mess I'm in with Harvey, what if I can't stay here? What if moving on can only happen by actually moving away?"

"Are you sure you have to do this for him? Why can't there be an alternative?"

"Because it's the only way I know how to show him that *he's* my father. He has been since I was twelve. It's the one last thing he's asking of me, and I owe him that," he stated, intertwining his fingers with mine in his lap.

"Don't they make Hallmark cards for that kind of thing?" I said lightheartedly, trying to break the tension. "I feel like a thoughtful handwritten letter could express some of what you're feeling. I'm not sure some kind of heist or drug bust or whatever you're planning, I'm not sure that conveys that same message."

"Harvey doesn't speak in cards," he replied with a gentle laugh. "I get what you're saying. I know this doesn't make sense. But if I do this, I can get out. If I don't, this won't end. Not with my father or with any of the people after Harvey."

"Now you're scaring me," I said seriously. "You sound like you're planning a mass murder."

"I'm not killing anyone," he smirked. "It's just karate. You know all about that. It's very effective," he teased.

"Cole, I'm serious. This whole thing concerns me."

"Do you remember that night when I gently put that guy to sleep at the bar and you were really angry with me? I told you I wasn't leaving you, right?"

"And then you slept on my steps that night, blood and all," I snickered.

"So my point is, I've never promised you something that wasn't true, right?"

I thought about his question seriously. He was always true to his word with me, right from the beginning. He never promised to be something he wasn't, and I always admired him for that. He knew we were such different people, but I believed every word he said to me. "I believe what you say," I confirmed.

"Then let me promise you something. I will take care of all of this, however it needs to be handled. I'll make it all go away and I'll never do another thing for Harvey again. But if it comes to the point that I have to leave, I need you to make a promise," he squeezed my hand. "Promise me you'll come with me. Promise me that if I say those words, that you won't hesitate. I have to know that you'll go with me."

The honest truth, as scary as all this was to me, I knew without a doubt in my mind that I would have no hesitation when it came to choosing Cole Mason. If the choice was being with him or not, I would certainly go with him. There would be no pause in that. No decision. No pros or cons list. I would simply choose *him.* But there was something unsettling inside of me – something leading me to believe that there was a possibility that I wouldn't even get that choice.

"I would go anywhere with you if that's what it took to be with you," I said honestly. "But you have to absolutely promise me that's how this ends. With us together. No alternative." I couldn't even say the words 'jail' or 'death' or anything along those lines. Certainly endings like that couldn't be possible. Not after all of these nights of loving each other, wrapped up and clinging to each other like we were all that was left under the stars. Surely there could be no other ending for us.

The only other fairytale I'd ever lived, the one with Ian – that was already this world's cruel way of reminding me of its power outside of whatever scenarios were in my head. I knew I didn't get to *choose* things that were otherwise just not meant to be. But if the choice was taken away from me altogether, I knew that would break me.

"I promise you there is no other ending to our story, Syd. This is it. You and me together. One way or another. No matter how this plays out, the end is still the same," he said reassuringly. "Just promise me you'll be there for me at the end of this. No matter what happens."

In some ways it felt like such a melodramatic conversation. I still didn't have a clue as to what Cole was even planning to do, nor did I know the seriousness of it. But I did understand that if Cole needed to start a new life somewhere, that would involve me, and my promise to him mattered.

I thought about his words for a moment. The way I fell for Cole – completely, unapologetically, without hesitation – I knew he would be worth any promise. I knew he was a man who would love me despite any circumstance – and I knew that was a man worth loving back. He was the kind of guy who admired who I was, and pushed me to be what I ultimately wanted to become – the kind of guy who could take my breath away with one look from the driver's side of his truck – the kind of guy who made me want to pour myself into the world to somehow make it better despite learning time and time again that the world wasn't as forgiving… I knew in that moment he was most certainly that kind of guy - the *falling* kind. The boy you chose because you know he will always love you back. The one who will fix whatever part of you is broken. The boy who would be willing to give it all up before ever leaving you behind. That was a man worth making that kind of promise to.

"I swear it," I whispered back. "Just you and me. At the end. Whatever happens."

CHAPTER 16

The next night Cole made plans for us to eat dinner at Harvey's. He actually said it was Harvey's idea to begin with, but I was skeptical. I didn't know Harvey at all. Other than a few courteous 'hellos' in passing while staying at Cole's house, I hadn't spent any time around him. I'd never even met his wife Sonita. I had nervous butterflies in my stomach after my shift at the clinic while I waited for Cole to pick me up.

I wore some capris and a loose top, trying to keep it casual. I bought a chocolate pie from a bakery by the clinic to offer for dessert. Cole knocked on my condo door right on time.

"I'm nervous," I admitted as he escorted me to his motorcycle. Ever since that first ride we took together on the bike, I was hooked. We hadn't gone on any long rides – it was mostly just from my place to his, and sometimes around the lake, but I loved it. The wind in my hair felt exhilarating and I loved the way his body felt tight underneath my grip.

He secured my pie into a carrier on the back of the seat and I smirked. It was quite amusing to watch such a big strong tattooed guy handle a delicate pie. We climbed onto his bike and I wrapped my arms around him as tight as I could and we made our way over to Harvey's.

We pulled into his driveway and Cole parked the bike. We knocked on the large green door of the cabin and a woman with long dark hair answered. She had silver strands in it towards the top of her head and I guessed she was in her early sixties, probably around Harvey's age. She had several long scars on her face and I wondered what story they held.

She smiled and her face softened as soon as she saw us, and she gave us a warm greeting. She hugged Cole and stepped back to take me in.

"You must be Sydney," she said politely, reaching out to give me a hug as well. It felt so genuine. "I've heard so many wonderful things about you. Cole can't keep quiet about it." I saw him blush as she said it. "We are so happy to have you here."

I thanked her politely and she led us through the house into the kitchen. Harvey was there at the counter, chopping some vegetables.

"Are you actually cooking tonight?" Cole razzed him, grabbing a carrot off his cutting board.

"I'm just on salad duty, Sonita made all of the pasta," Harvey replied, winking at his wife. I could tell how much he cared for her just by the way he looked at her. I wasn't sure how to feel about Harvey; he obviously made a lot of bad, dangerous choices, probably on a daily basis. But the way he seemed to care for his family, it seemed so admirable. To love the same woman for forty years – that was beautiful to me, no matter how bad of a guy he was. And the way he took Cole in as a child, that was enough to make me want to believe that deep down he had plenty of goodness in him.

"Can I help you with anything?" I offered politely.

"Just tell me what you want to drink for dinner," Sonita replied warmly. "I have wine, lemonade, iced tea?"

"Lemonade would be wonderful, thank you," I answered. Cole helped her fill up our cups and she pulled a couple dishes out of the oven, motioning for us to head towards the dining room table.

"So you work at the vet clinic?" Sonita asked as we sat down and served up our plates.

"Yes, I've been there for a few years now, that's what I studied in college," I explained. I wasn't sure how much Cole told them about me.

"And your plans are to open up an animal rescue?" she continued. *Okay, so apparently he told them quite a bit.*

"Well, eventually… Hopefully," I smiled. "It's a lot of work, and I need space. I'm not quite there yet. There are still some animals I've never even worked on yet. I need a lot more experience."

"You're a bright girl," Harvey chimed in. "I bet you could accomplish all of that, with the right resources." He said it with an endearing tone, but his choice of words still made it sound more like a business conversation.

I took a bite of pasta and it was amazing. It had a light cream sauce and sautéed vegetables. There were pieces of chicken, sausage, and shrimp, and it was one of the best homemade meals I'd ever eaten.

"So how did you two meet?" I asked curiously, making conversation.

"I won her in a poker game when I was nineteen," Harvey replied quickly with a huge grin. I did not expect that answer. "She was going steady with a guy I knew, and I hated him. His name was Burton, what kind of a name is that?"

Sonita playfully rolled her eyes. "It was a fine name," she scoffed.

"Well he was no good for her. It made me crazy. I would see him around town, flirting with other women. He didn't deserve her," he said nobly.

"So how did she become a poker bet?" I questioned.

"I was playing cards with some guys in town and he wanted to join in," Harvey explained. "He was real cocky like he was something better than us. I told him the buy-in was too high, he couldn't afford it. He told me he'd put anything up, that's how confident he was. So I told him he had to throw in the girl. The bastard actually agreed to it."

Sonita took a sip of her drink, shaking her head. “These men were mere boys,” she teased.

“Long story short, I won the poker game,” Harvey continued. “Best pot I ever won.”

“And that’s it? You became his over a bet?” I smirked. It was quiet an interesting story.

“Not at all, I turned him down,” Sonita replied loudly with a smile. “I couldn’t believe his audacity, to think I was somehow his property all because of a poker game. I told him to get lost.”

“So what did you do?” I asked towards Harvey.

“I didn’t go away,” he smirked.

Ah, now I see where Cole got his persistence from.

“We were married by the next year,” Sonita continued with a huge grin. “And he still won’t get lost when I tell him to, so I guess this is it for me.” They looked at each other and you could see their love in their expressions.

“I see you and Cole together, and I recognize that look,” Harvey said with a gentle smile. “I’m realizing that Cole has no plans to disappear from your life. So I guess the real reason you’re here tonight though is to find out what he’s up to, right?” Harvey said directly, completely changing the subject.

“I get worried about him,” I said truthfully, sipping on my drink as a distraction from him being able to read my face. Honestly I so badly wanted to talk them both out of whatever they had planned.

"There's a lot you're better off not knowing," Harvey began in a serious tone, "but some back story may be helpful to you… To both of you."

I glanced between Cole and Harvey, wondering if Cole knew everything he was about to tell us.

"There are conversations we've never had, Cole, and I think we're at a point where this needs to be said. Sonita and I had a boy once," he said with some emotion in his voice. He reached his arm over and rested his hand on top of Sonita's, which was resting on the table. "He was nine years old when he was killed by a drunk driver."

The emotion in his voice got me choked up as he said it. "I'm so sorry to hear that," I replied quietly.

"He was the greatest boy. He was good in school and he loved to build things. There's a creek up the way," he continued, pointing back behind the cabin, "and he made the greatest forts over there. Just a young boy, exploring the woods God gave him, skipping rocks, climbing trees… as innocent as each one of us is born."

"How have you not told me this before?" Cole questioned. He almost looked hurt that he didn't know such personal information about Harvey.

“Because it breaks her heart every time I bring it up,” Harvey said emotionally. I could see slow tears falling down Sonita’s face as he spoke. “A mother losing her child, there is no greater heartbreak than that. She cried every single day for years. We tried to have another child, but it didn’t happen. She was full of such sorrow and I thought it would break us.” I could see him squeeze her hand as he continued talking. “But then all of that changed. There was mischief out behind the cabins. My tools kept going missing and there were small footprints all about.” Sonita’s mouth curled up into a slight smile despite her slow tears.

“It was the first time her face didn’t look like heartbreak,” Harvey continued. “You were staying in one of the trailers up the road with your dad and his sister. You were always sneaking around the compound, probably hiding from his fists I imagine. But Sonita would occasionally hear whispers from the trees, and splashes in the water. Her whole face lit up. It put life back in her soul. The giant hole she had in her heart, it slowly began to fill back up. It was real gradual at first, but then she’d hear laughter back in the woodshed and her own happiness grew from that sound. One night, after your daddy was taken away, I heard you creeping around the garage. I started talking about the constellations, aloud to myself on the chance you were listening. Sonita saw you sit down on the back porch out of my view, and you were listening to me, staring up at the night sky."

Cole's eyes looked misty, and I couldn't believe this was the first time he'd ever heard this story.

"I came in that night," Harvey continued, "and Sonita was crying, but she looked so far away from sadness. She had this huge grin on her face and I knew something had changed in her. That hole was gone. It's not that she stopped missing Samuel, but that boy in the woods – his laughter – *your* laughter – it restored her. God brought her a boy. Not the one she lost years before, but a boy someone else lost."

A slow tear slid down my cheek and I wiped it away. I looked over at Cole, trying to gauge how he felt by the look on his face. His eyes still looked moist, but he didn't seem to know what to say.

"Why didn't you tell me this before?" Cole questioned.

"I never wanted you to feel like you were just a replacement to us," Sonita said towards Cole. "You were never taking his place. If you'd known about Samuel, you would've thought that's what happened, that you were replacing him. But you were so much more. You deserved to believe you were the only one."

"I still don't understand why you didn't tell me you had a son," Cole said quietly. "Maybe

I wouldn't have understood it as a child, but later I would have. You should have told me."

"There's a lot you don't know," Harvey said empathetically. "I did it to protect you."

"Protect me from what?" Cole asked, raising his voice.

"I know it all needs to come out now," Harvey replied, nodding his head. "You may still not understand it all. But you should know."

"What should I know?" Cole questioned with a hint of anger in his voice. He looked back and forth between Harvey and Sonita, and I could tell his frustration was growing.

"You've always asked me how I knew your father," Harvey said softly.

"And you always gave me some bullshit answer that he was some kind of poker acquaintance you couldn't get rid of," Cole sneered.

"I did it to protect you," Harvey repeated, as if that alone was supposed to make more sense. "He's not just an old acquaintance, Cole. Your father is the man that killed my son."

CHAPTER 17

Cole angrily slammed his fist down on the dining room table and I jumped. I could see his mind racing and I feared for a moment that his anger would get the best of him and he would again become unrecognizable to me.

"I don't believe you," Cole said, narrowing his eyes at Harvey.

"I didn't know it was him for many years," Harvey clarified. "The pieces didn't fit at first. It was a hit and run, so there was limited information. Back when it happened I had no clue. I didn't even really know your dad back then, he was so much younger than me. Occasionally he'd play in some poker games I was a part of, and he even worked in the bike shop here and there. But he was always in and out of prison. It was mostly petty stuff, drugs, conversion, theft."

"Then how did you find out about the hit and run?" Cole questioned. I sat there in complete silence.

"When you were twelve, that's when your daddy was put away for ten years for that arson charge. He got mixed up with the wrong people and he got busted for that," Harvey explained. "That's when we took you in. I knew he'd be gone a long time and you needed someone. When he finally got released, you were a man already. You were twenty-two – not that young, scared boy he left behind all those years before. You refused to see him when he got out."

"There was no reason to," Cole said sternly. "The only memories I have of that man are of his fists and his slurred, angry speech. He has no claim to me."

"You set him up after he got out," Harvey said quietly.

"Damn straight I did, he deserved it," Cole replied angrily. "How did you know it was me?"

"I facilitated the entire thing in some way," Harvey answered hesitantly. "When your father got out, he insisted he would draw you away from me. He didn't want you working for me and insisted he had some information that would make you turn on me. He said I deserved it for taking you away from him."

"None of this is making sense," Cole said irritably.

"I set up the job knowing your father would have a trail to it, because those were the old boys he used to work with. I knew the operation would get busted, it was intended to," Harvey stated with a steady voice. "I wanted proof of your loyalty. I wanted to know if you would try to cover it for him or if you would throw him into the flames."

"Why would you need proof of that?" Cole exclaimed, slamming his fist on the table again. "I've felt so much guilt the last two years over putting him away. I did it out of spite, just because

I could. Don't you realize how heavily that's weighed on me?"

"I do," Harvey confirmed solemnly.

"Then why didn't you say something then?" Cole huffed. "Why did you ask me to take the heat for him? You made up that entire story, like he was going to be joining the business with you and you needed him. What was all that?"

"A test," Harvey said directly.

"What test for you have I ever failed?" Cole said loudly with expressive arms, standing up from the table. "Why would I ever side with that piece of shit man who has never done anything for me? What did I have to prove? What hadn't *I* proved to you by then?" Cole's anger was all over his face. "I just wanted him out of the picture! And then you asked me to take his sentence? That's not a test Harvey. That's some bullshit penance you wanted held over me to give you power."

"I wanted *you* in jail, Cole," Harvey admitted. "I honestly thought out of your loyalty to me, you would do it because I asked you to." I looked over at Cole who just stood there, shaking his head in disbelief.

"That's sick," Cole said through gritted teeth.

"That's the only place you would've been protected from what was supposed to happen," Harvey replied cryptically. "I had received correspondence from your father when he got out of jail. The message simply said he'd already taken one of my boys from me, with a promise to take my other boy. *You.* I couldn't let that happen."

"I still don't understand what you're saying," Cole breathed.

"I wanted you in jail for something petty, just briefly, so there was no way you would be a suspect for what I had planned to happen. I'd made arrangements for your father to 'disappear' the following day. I vowed that your father would take his last breath before anything happened to you. I set up a bad job, hoping you would be picked up for it to get you out of the picture so you couldn't be tied to your father's disappearance in any way. But instead, when things went bad you pinned your father. That messed with my plans, but I thought if I could convince you to take the heat, I could still proceed with what I wanted to do, but you didn't go for it, and your father was sent back in."

"So what now? What does this all mean right *now*? He's been released again. He's already out. What are we doing?" Cole asked Harvey. "And don't you lie to me about anything else. Just tell me what we're going to do."

I still sat in silence, trying to follow everything being said. This was such a messed up situation on so many levels.

"Your father needs the justice he deserves, for everything he's done," Harvey stated calmly. "The guy he's working for, Burton McClellan…"

"Wait, Burton from the poker game? The guy who gave up Sonita?" I interrupted, trying to make sure I understood the connection.

"Yes, that Burton," Harvey continued, "he's been shorting our payments and causing trouble. He's been interfering with our business, and you know I don't tolerate that. The fact that your dad is mixed up with him too, that just makes this all the more easier to rectify. Burton has six hundred thousand dollars that belong to me, you know that," he said towards Cole.

Cole nodded in return.

"So the job is two-fold. We get back the money, and I make sure your father is permanently out of the picture," Harvey stated.

"You're going to murder him?" I shrieked. "I feel like I shouldn't be hearing this. I don't want any part of this," I said nervously, shaking my head.

Cole looked at me with apologetic eyes, and it felt like there was so much he wanted to say to me, but he didn't speak. I hoped once we were alone he would be more willing to talk all of this over with me. Hopefully he wanted no part in this as well, but his expression told me otherwise.

"I know you mean a great deal to Cole," Harvey said to me softly. "But he's not safe right now. His father wants revenge, as do the people he works for. And if there's a target on him, there's a target on you." I noticed Sonita slowly raise her left hand and touch the scars on her face. I could see so much sadness in her eyes. "Sydney, this is the best thing for you both. We will finish this now, and he will be set free. Otherwise there is no end for the violence that surrounds him."

"I still don't understand," I said quietly.

"One of two things will happen," Harvey replied simply. "If the job goes well, like I plan, I'll get the money I'm owed and Cole's father will be paid off. He will disappear. I have no plans to harm him Sydney, I just simply need him to vanish. There's a difference."

"And the other scenario?" Cole asked, still maintaining his stern expression.

"If he doesn't take the money, then his disappearance will be forced," Harvey replied hesitantly. "But one way or another, he needs to be out of the picture."

"What if I won't help you? What then?" Cole demanded, shaking his head.

"That's not a risk worth taking," Harvey answered. "Cole, so many things... The scars you have, the motorcycle accident years ago – none of the things you've been through were accidental. They were all done intentionally. Your father has had people working for him the whole time he's been in prison, and he's been connected to Burton since before he even went in. The blackmail threats I've received, those won't end until your father is removed from all of this. Those people are all out for me, Cole, but you know they'll go through you to make that happen. They know hurting you hurts me, and they aren't afraid to do that. Not even your own father."

I thought back to the night Cole followed me home from that West Cove dive bar. I thought he was just being protective and crazy, insinuating someone would hurt me just to hurt him. Now in this conversation, I saw Harvey treat him in the same overprotective way. And Sonita's face – that was clearly an attempt at someone's retaliation against Harvey. I suddenly felt less safe now than I ever had since meeting Cole.

"This is it, Harvey," Cole said firmly. "This is the very last thing I will be a part of. But only with your guarantee that I'm out after this. Completely. Forever."

"You have my word on that Cole," Harvey agreed. "This is it. You will be released from all of this. But this goes down tomorrow night, so there isn't any time for wavering. You participate, and this is all over."

Cole looked at me and I didn't know what to say. I knew there was so much I still didn't know. But I didn't *want* to know. All I wanted was for things to go back to how they were – the last couple months we spent splashing in the summer sun, and learning about each other under perfect, starlit skies. Somehow in an instant we seemed so far away from that and I hated it. I knew I would give anything to get that back – that's what I wanted.

"I'm taking Sydney home," Cole said bluntly, reaching out for my hand.

"What about the lovely pie you brought?" Sonita replied warmly.

"You guys enjoy that on your own," Cole said dismissively. "Syd, come on." I stood up from the table and reached out for his hand. "I'll be by tomorrow," he added towards Harvey, and that was it. Within sixty seconds we were headed back to my condo on his motorcycle.

"What are you thinking?" Cole said softly as we entered my house.

"Honestly, I don't know," I replied. "I don't understand any of this. I just want to wish it all away."

"Can we go up to the roof?" he asked with sweet eyes and an exhausted smile. "I want to lay by the fire with you."

I nodded and we headed to the rooftop, stretching out on the sofa next to the fire pit like we'd done so many other nights.

"I feel like I'm losing you," I said quietly, tracing my fingers lazily across his chest.

"What happened to our promise? Me and you at the end, no matter what, right?" He grabbed my hand and pulled it up to his mouth, gently kissing it. "That hasn't changed."

"Do you ever wish you hadn't met me?" I asked honestly. It was a valid question. Maybe I was trying to change who he was. Maybe he wouldn't be caught up in all of this if I wasn't trying so hard to pull him away from it all.

"I'll never have that thought," he replied shaking his head. "Look, I know all of this is messy. It's ugly and it's complicated. I know that. And yeah, I wish I never got you involved in any of this. I hate myself for that. But not at the cost of giving you up. I knew when we met, I wasn't good enough for you. I wasn't worthy of your love then, I knew that. But for some crazy reason, you chose me anyway, just on the promise that I would be good enough for you eventually. I know I'm still trying, but don't give up on me."

"I can't give up on you," I shrugged. "Trust me, this would be so much easier if I could. But I feel like I'm making this worse for you. Like you have one more thing to deal with. I just wish this was all.... simpler."

"Boring people have boring love stories," he snickered, squeezing my hand. "Just think of the story we'll tell our children someday."

"Geez, you move quick," I teased. "Who knew we'd go from tacos to felonies to planning a family."

"I didn't say the kids would belong to us jointly. I meant you could tell your kids and I would tell mine," he said with a sarcastic laugh. "Why would I want to have children with you someday? They would come out all smart and good. Bleh."

"But they'll also have tattoos by the time they're ten and a vocab full of curse words," I teased back. "They'll be well balanced."

He leaned down and kissed me, interrupting my smile. It amazed me the way he could talk about our future together when I wasn't confident we'd even survive another forty-eight hours.

"I'm going to fix all of this tomorrow," he said softly as he pulled away from me. He stared at me as he said it and I believed him. "I'll go to Harvey's and do what I have to do. One way or another, tomorrow will be the last day of my old life. The entire life I knew before I met you – all of that will be left behind and then it's just you and me."

I kissed him again, memorizing the way his lips felt against mine – the way his hands felt as they grazed my skin – the way he breathed in the silence that surrounded us.

"So I just wait until you call me and tell me it's all over?" I asked curiously.

"Hopefully," he replied quietly.

"Cole, I want something better than 'hopefully,' you're scaring me."

"If something happens, don't freak out," he explained. "I'll call you when I can, but I'm just saying if you don't hear from me right away, don't panic."

"Cole, what are you saying?"

"I'm just trying to prepare you," he said, touching my face. "These things don't always go how they're supposed to. I'm just saying don't panic right away if you don't hear something. If things go bad, I may not be able to contact you right away."

"Cole, what's your part in all this? How can things go bad, what does that mean for you?"

"I'll be okay, I promise," he said reassuringly. "I just don't want you coming by Harvey's or something trying to find me if I'm unable to call you tomorrow night. Not until everything clears. Look, if you don't hear from me right away, or by Thursday morning let's say, go to Antonio's. I'll get communication to him somehow, only if I can't reach you for some reason. I'll find some way to keep you in the loop, but just be patient. That can be our backup plan."

"It starts and ends with tacos, how ironic," I said lightly. My stomach was in knots but I was trying to suppress my worry.

"Nothing's ending," he said sincerely. "It's all just beginning."

CHAPTER 18

Cole and I slept under the stars one more night, as if everything was ordinary. But I swear he held me a little tighter and his lips lingered a little bit longer against mine.

I had the early shift at the clinic, and I hated peeling away from him before the sun was even up. It felt like the world's cruel way of reminding us that there were limitations to what we got in life – a reminder that time could in no way be controlled by people.

I kissed his sleepy lips and I could feel his face turn up into a smile. "I'll wait to hear from you," I tried saying confidently, though I'm sure he picked up on the slight waiver in my voice. I knew he would let himself out once he got up and around.

"Syd," he said softly, grabbing my hand as I began to turn and head out, "you're the girl I'm going to love forever."

My eyes filled with tears and I gently squeezed his hand. "See you soon," I whispered, unsure of when that was. I left quietly and headed to the clinic.

I was on edge for most of the day, despite it being a pretty routine work day. It was strange not to have Sam around, I still needed to get used to that. Oh what I would give to have her present through all of this. I felt so alone despite such familiar surroundings and I hated it. Dr. Nikki asked twice if there was something I wanted to talk about, but I declined conversation both times even though I had so much weighing on my mind.

At the end of my shift, I popped my head into Dr. Nikki's office and she called me in, asking me to have a seat.

"I think I know what's going on," she said as I sat down in one of the yellow arm chairs sitting in front of her dark wooden desk.

"I can't imagine you do," I said lightheartedly.

"Fall semester starts this week," she began, clearly not letting me out of some type of discussion. "You changed your plans. I know Washington changed for you, but what else? Is this some kind of remorse about not heading back to school? A lot of people go through that after they graduate while they're trying to figure out what they want to do."

"I don't know," I said honestly. "I really haven't given it much thought recently. But I know deep down I've been struggling with what to do. Sam had such a direct plan laid out, and she's off doing that, you know? I feel like no one tells you what it's really like after you graduate. Four years of school and I'm in the same place. It's like I'm not moving. But I'm happy, so that's something, right? But so much has changed over the last couple months."

"Is this about that boy you've been running around with?" she asked with a sly grin. "Boys like that have a way of messing with a girl's plans."

"I know," I smirked. "But my plan was cloudy when we met. If anything I feel like he's trying to encourage me to go after what I ultimately want. But I just don't feel ready. I feel like on my own I'm just *not* ready."

"So let someone help you," she said compassionately. "What do you want?"

"I don't know, a normal life? I never thought that would be too much to ask for," I sighed. "I just want a *simple* life. I want to eventually open a rescue where I feel like I can make a difference. I want to watch the sun rise and set. I want land and trees and a garden and animals everywhere."

"I completely understand that dream," Dr. Nikki said sympathetically. "You can have all that you know. You have what it takes."

"Yeah, but can I do that here? I can't fit very many animals in my two-story condo," I said lightheartedly. "I just don't know what direction to go. Do I get more education? Do I work for someone else's rescue first to become more prepared? Do I even have to have an answer to all this right now?" I laughed.

"The funny thing about life is that it decides so much for you," she replied warmly. "I followed a guy here when I was twenty-three. We were going to be ski instructors and live out our days on the tops of mountains."

"Really?" I asked surprised. She'd never mentioned anything about that before. "So what happened?"

"I found a dog on the side of the highway with a new litter of puppies, and I vowed I would take care of all seven of them. Meanwhile the guy I was with found a brunette. So I quickly learned when one thing ends, another begins," she snickered. "I knew then I wanted to go back to school for Veterinary Science and that was my calling. I know it's cliché, but always go with your gut, and the rest works itself out. I'm a firm believer that's always the answer."

"Thank you," I replied sincerely. "For everything. You've done so much for me. Whatever direction I decide to go, I just want you to know how thankful and appreciative I am of everything."

I said goodbye to her and headed back to my condo, replaying that conversation. It seemed like weird timing to have that discussion, but I was grateful we did.

As I walked into my house, I noticed a small box with a note on my end table. I picked up the card and read it.

Just to make sure you don't forget our promise.

I opened the box and pulled out a beautiful thin silver necklace chain with a plain silver ring on it. The inscription inside the ring immediately caught my eye. *Just you and me.* It was simple, but yet so perfect to me.

I took a quick shower and tied my hair up, putting the necklace on as soon as I was dressed. I loved everything about it. I couldn't wait to thank him later.

I knew I needed some kind of plan for the rest of the evening. Sitting around waiting for Cole to call would eat my brain. I needed some kind of distraction.

I talked to Sam on the phone for about a half hour. She was all settled into her new place in Oregon and she sounded so happy. I didn't want to bog her down with my current frustrations, so I glazed over my recap of all that had happened since she left and let her gush about how amazing her new campus was and how excited she was for all the change she had going on.

Afterwards I dialed Brandt, and he agreed to go out to a movie with me. I hoped that would shut off my thoughts about Cole and whatever he was up to.

My big mistake of the night was allowing Brandt to pick the movie. A two and a half hour superhero flick was not what I had in mind. After the movie we hit up a local Mexican restaurant for a late dinner.

"So what did you think about the flick?" Brandt asked as we waited for our order.

"It felt… long," I said honestly with a laugh. "So many jumpsuits."

"Oh come on, you used to love those kinds of movies, what happened?" he said animatedly.

"No, Ian used to love those movies. And I loved Ian, so that's how that happened," I chuckled. It was a rarity for me to bring up Ian's name so casually, but it just spilled out.

"I can't believe you just said his name while smiling at the same time," he replied sincerely. "It's been a long time." His expression was warm and friendly. So many times in my sorrow and hurt I forgot that Brandt also lost his best friend that same day. Yet somehow Brandt never blamed me for what happened, despite all of the guilt I carried from it. "You know, I never thought I'd be happy for you to replace Ian. Better yet, I never thought I'd witness it after what you put yourself through, blaming yourself like you did. But I'm proud of you, Syd." He looked at me with such a genuine expression.

"I still go through the what-ifs," I admitted, "but I finally realized the rest of the world didn't stop spinning just because my small portion of it felt like it did. I feel like I messed up in so many ways. But then time moves on, and anyone outside of that fragment of my life, they didn't feel anything like we did, right? It seemed like in an instant, the whole world crashed – but then everyone else around us kept moving along. I couldn't wrap my mind around that for the longest time. First my mom, then Ian. I just couldn't understand how this big life event took place, and there I was – left screaming into the wind for no one to hear. But then, someone hears you. And they can't fix it or eradicate that event from existing – but they hear you. And somehow you realize that's enough to keep moving."

Brandt stared at me with a somewhat bewildered expression. "That's deep for fried taquito conversation," he teased as our food was set down in front of us. I smirked as he said it, finding it ironic just how many deep conversations I had over tacos the last couple months.

We ate our food and our conversation lightened, and we laughed and joked like so many times before.

Around ten, the restaurant finally kicked us out so they could close for the night. As Brandt and I parted ways, I pulled him in for a big hug. "Thank you. For your friendship. Everything," I said, finally releasing him.

"Are you dying? Do you have cancer?" he joked, raising a brow at me. "You're so serious tonight. What's going on?"

"Nothing," I said dismissively. "I'm just a little on edge. I'm fine."

"Do you want to talk about it? I mean you just had three hours to bring it up, but I can spare some more time if you need it," he teased.

"No, I know you have an early morning tomorrow. I'm fine, I promise," I lied. The truth was, I didn't want to go home. I didn't want to sleep. I didn't want one second of silence to think about Cole.

Brandt and I said goodnight and I climbed back in my car. I wondered where else I could even go by myself at this time of night. All of the restaurants and coffee shops were closed already, and I had no interest in going into one of the loud, chaotic casinos downtown. As I headed towards my condo, a small Irish pub caught my eye. The parking lot had some cars, but it didn't seem overly busy. *A bar.* Probably the only place to show up to alone on a weeknight when you had nowhere else to go.

I pulled into the lot, not totally sure what I was doing there. I had no better ideas though, so despite my better judgment, I went inside. I was still on the Mountain Ridge side at least, so it's not like I was someplace dangerous.

I opened the large wooden door and a few heads turned, but otherwise no one even noticed me. I sat on a barstool up against the middle of the bar and a woman in her fifties asked what I wanted.

"A Shirley Temple would be great," I shrugged, not really in the mood to even drink that.

"Are you underage or something?" she laughed, looking confused by my drink order.

"No, I just don't drink," I sighed.

"You realize this is a bar, right?" she replied with a sarcastic tone. "That's pretty much the opposite of our mission statement."

"Drinking has never done me any favors," I said honestly. "Although of all nights, I probably need one." My hands were shaking and my entire body felt full of anxiety. All I wanted was a phone call or a text. *Something* to tell me Cole was okay. I hated waiting.

"This favor's on me," she responded, sliding me a glass of clear liquid. I didn't suspect it was water. Without thinking about it, I quickly slugged it down, ready to gag it all back up again as it burned through my throat. I wasn't even sure what kind of alcohol it was, but if fire was a clear liquid, I would've guessed that. I literally felt like it was burning through my trachea.

"Too harsh?" she snickered, clearly amused by my painful reaction. "Try this, there's juice in it. That should help."

I slugged down the next drink, thankful for the sweetness of the pineapple juice as it hit my lips. The drink still wasn't good by any means, but it was far better than what I started with.

"It's Sydney, right?" a male voice said from behind me. I turned on my chair to see a familiar guy I couldn't quite place. "No boyfriend tonight?"

I studied his face, trying to figure out where I knew him from. It wasn't coming to me.

"Ridge City Chad from the bonfire, remember?" he said with a slight laugh, lightening the mood.

"Right, the only other Ridge City hanging out in West Cove," I smirked, kind of relieved it was him and not someone else from the bonfire that night. "What a stupid nickname."

"What are you drinking tonight?" he questioned, sitting on the barstool next to me.

"I ordered a Shirley Temple, but she gave me something toxic instead," I said pointing to the two empty glasses in front of me. The bartender was currently pouring a drink for two guys towards the end of the bar. She finally came back our way and asked what we wanted.

"You interested in some whiskey?" Chad asked with a raised brow.

"The girl says she doesn't drink," the bartender scoffed.

"I don't," I confirmed, realizing I looked like an idiot for stating that in a bar.

"Why not? What's the worst that can happen?" the bartender shrugged.

"Last time I drank I killed my boyfriend," I said quietly. I don't know why that came out of my mouth.

"You killed that guy? With all the muscles and the tattoos?" Chad said in a panicked voice.

"No," I shook my head, wrongly amused by his misunderstanding. "The guy before that."

"I'll get you that Shirley Temple," the bartender said quickly with big eyes.

"No, I should probably just get out of here," I shrugged, getting up from my barstool. "I don't know why I came here."

"Do you need to talk or something?" Chad asked politely. "I'm meeting someone here in a few minutes, but if you need an ear…"

The door of the bar swung open at that moment and a tall blonde in a low cut tank top walked in. *Britt.* Seeing Cole's ex tonight was not what I needed at the moment.

"No thanks," I said through a fake smile. "Nice to see you again. Good luck with that," I added, motioning towards the door. I quickly grabbed my purse and made a loop around the room and outside the front door so that I wouldn't have to cross paths with her. The cool evening air hit me in the face and made my head feel a little less cloudy, but I still felt unlike my usual self. Words at the bar were just falling out of my mouth, to strangers no less – what was that? I wasn't sure why I went in there in the first place. I just wanted to be anywhere but home, but that wasn't helping. I felt like I wanted an escape from all the thoughts circling around in my head, but I should've known better. Alcohol only made things worse for me, never better.

I drove slowly down the block to my condo, thankful I was so close. It was only two drinks, I knew that, but my head still didn't feel right. Suddenly now I was ready for sleep – something to take my mind off of Cole tonight. I parked my car and walked up my steps, slowly turning the key in my door. I somberly walked in, closing the door behind me, thankful there was only one dim light left on in my living room. Bright lights sounded the opposite of comforting at the moment. I simply wanted to climb in bed and forget this entire day.

As I set my purse down on the small table in my entryway, I immediately felt a strange draft of air, causing the hairs on my arm to prickle. I glanced across the room through the dim light past my dining room table.

Was my kitchen window open?

I flicked on the living room light, trying to figure out where the air was coming from. I didn't recall opening any windows before I left for the movies, and I was pretty sure I would've noticed it earlier if Cole opened them up for some reason before he let himself out.

Before I could process anything, two cold, strong hands reached out from the darkness behind me, pressing over my mouth. They felt rough and unfamiliar.

I could feel warm breath on the back of my neck as a deep, unrecognizable voice spoke into my ear. "Don't scream."

CHAPTER 19

My entire body went numb and I felt sick and dizzy all at once. My eyes widened and filled with tears.

The hands covering my mouth stayed firmly on me, and the strong tattooed arms wrapped around me didn't loosen their grip.

"I promise I'm not here to hurt you," the voice said from behind me, "but you need to promise me you won't scream."

Honestly, even if I wanted to scream, I wasn't entirely confident any sound would come out. I was so completely petrified, unable to even think straight.

I slowly nodded my head in agreement and he loosened his grasp.

The strong man still held me, restricting my movement, but he maneuvered his body in front of me. He was tall, well over six feet, and his face looked tired and weathered. He had really short, light brown hair with a military-style cut, and flecks of grey showed through his facial hair stubble.

His eyes looked directly into mine as he slowly moved his hand from my mouth. They were a soft blue-green color and they reminded me of Cole. *Cole. This man had Cole's eyes.*

"I'm not going to hurt you," the man replied softly. "Do you know who I am?"

"I… I think so," I stammered quietly. I wasn't sure if that was something to admit or not, but my thought process was shattered.

"My name is Grady, and I believe you know my son Cole." He continued to stare at me as he spoke, probably still wondering if I planned to scream for help at any point. Instead I just slowly nodded. "I imagine you've heard a thing or two about me?"

"A little," I squeaked, unsure of what else to say.

"Probably nothing good," he replied quietly.

"Cole's not here," I said nervously, unsure what he was expecting tonight. I was hoping that may be enough to make him leave.

"I know that," he stated calmly. "I'm just here to pass along a message for him."

I studied his face, wondering why he was truly here. My entire body was tense and I wanted to throw up my nerves.

"Did you see him tonight?" I asked reluctantly.

"I did," Grady said calmly. "He wanted me to tell you he has to lay low for a bit. Don't turn on the TV. If you do, don't panic. Don't believe everything you hear, and don't freak out about it. Just go to Antonio's tomorrow."

The Antonio's part led me to believe that he really had talked to Cole at some point. How else would he have known that was part of our plan?

“Why did he send you? I don’t believe he would’ve sent you,” I said quietly. It didn’t make sense. He hated his father, and from what Harvey said, his father was working for the other side. His presence here didn’t add up.

“What all do you know about me?” He narrowed his eyes at me, and I felt less afraid of him as he spoke. There was some softness to his eyes, something that made him seem less threatening. But I still knew from Cole and Harvey that he wasn’t someone to take lightly.

“I don’t really know anything,” I stated truthfully.

“What has Cole told you about me?” he asked bluntly. He loosened his grip on me again and motioned me towards the couch.

“I don’t know, not much,” I said nervously.

“I need your honesty,” Grady said calmly, sitting down next to me on the couch. “I know you’re scared right now, but we need to have a conversation.”

“He only told me one thing about you,” I said quietly. “He said you were cruel. That’s all he remembers of you.” I probably should’ve softened my words, but I didn’t have anything else to say. The truth was, that was the single only detail Cole had ever mentioned. “He was just a boy,” I added with emotion weighing heavy in my throat. My eyes welled up and I still felt frozen. "He was just a little boy," I whispered again.

"I *was* cruel," he said softly, nodding his head. He continued to stare at me. "I was not a good father. I was young, and I had no help. I didn't know what to do with him. I was so worried about myself, trying to make a living, trying to get ahead. I know I wasn't a good father. I wasn't what he needed. I know that."

These admissions from Grady were completely unexpected. But then again, I wondered what his true motives were for being here. I felt like he was baiting me into some kind of trap, and I wasn't sure I could trust him.

"I sent him letters," Grady continued with a hint of nostalgia in his voice. "Once I sobered up in prison, I finally saw what a terrible person I had become. I regretted it. All of it. I wrote him letters, trying to reach out to him. I didn't want his forgiveness, and as a child I didn't expect his understanding. But I wanted him to know that I knew - - that I knew I'd messed up, and that I'd failed him. I just wanted him to know I knew that."

"He never told me you tried contacting him," I said skeptically, wondering if he was making it all up.

"He didn't know. I sent the letters to Harvey. I got word from other inmates coming and going that Harvey had taken him in. I didn't really know him, he lived in the cabin up the street from a trailer I was staying in at the time. I didn't know where else to send the letters. For a long time, I had no idea Harvey wasn't giving my correspondence to him."

"How do you know that now?" I questioned, wondering if I would be able to decipher his lies from truths.

"When I got out of prison a couple years back, I tried to reconnect with Cole. I knew he would be angry with me, I expected that. Even if he threw all my letters away, I still expected him to read at least one. But the only exchange we had when I was released, it was brief – he told me I was a liar. He didn't believe I spent one second thinking about him while I was put away. He obviously didn't get one single letter I sent. A few months back he was in jail, briefly, and we crossed paths. He still didn't believe Harvey would do such a thing because of course Harvey denied all of it."

I studied his face as he spoke, trying to determine how genuine he seemed. His words sounded sincere, but his face looked like one of those men who could easily change their expression to fit the mood of the situation. He could easily lie to me and I wouldn't be able to tell the difference.

"You look like you don't believe me," he said, calling me out. Apparently he was good at reading people.

"It doesn't matter if I believe you or not," I shrugged. "You're trying to tell me Harvey is the bad guy and you're not? You abandoned your own child. I have no sympathy for you. Why would Cole send you here?" I asked directly. I wanted him to just cut to the chase.

"Because Cole finally realized the truth," he said in a frustrated tone. "A lot came out tonight. Burton had been blackmailing Harvey all these years, but it finally all came to a head tonight. Harvey's kept so many things from Cole all these years. Things about his mother – Harvey was the one supplying her with all the drugs that destroyed her. She still lives in town, walking around as high as a kite, and Cole didn't even know it. Even truths about what really happened to Harvey's boy, those came out as well – Burton knew it all. And it wasn't the same story Harvey told Cole. It all came out tonight. Cole knows the truth. He finally knows we're not on such different sides after all."

"How do I know any of that's true?" I asked straightforwardly.

"How else would I know about you?"

I stared at him with questioning eyes. He did have a valid point there, but from the way Harvey and Cole made it sound, it was possible someone else could know that information. Maybe someone followed me one night, or maybe someone picked up on where Cole had been staying most of the summer. "Prove it," I stated, crossing my arms. Any fear I had of this man faded, and now I was just pissed. He came into my house, intimidating me, possibly lying to me… I had no reason to trust him, and no reason to help him.

"He told me when things got messy tonight, to find you and get word to you that he was completely okay," he explained.

"Why didn't you start with that?" I sneered.

"Geez, the one thing he didn't tell me was that you were such a ball buster," he smirked. "He said you would at least hear me out. He said you were *good*. He was very clear on that. He said you would give me a chance because of your goodness. He said you would at least listen to me. He was afraid you would see the news and you would panic. Just ignore what you hear and go to Antonio's in the morning. That's why he sent me, to make sure you knew that."

"What happened tonight?" I asked bluntly, hoping for some answers. I still wasn't sure I could trust him, despite all of the information he was relaying to me.

"That's a story for Cole to tell you," he said warily. "I have no place in his business. I'm just here to do right by him for once in my life because I promised him I would. That's it. I'm not here to fix the past, or to change his mind about me for the future. I have no right to do so. I just want you to know he's okay, and I want you to know how grateful I am that he has a girl like you. One who is *good*. One who cares about him despite their own circumstance. You are the only thing that can make this better for him, Sydney," he stated. "Everyone in Cole's life has given up on him. Every single person. His mother chose her addiction over him, and I chose my pride. Harvey chose power over him, and used him to gain what he wanted. His relationships gave up on him, everyone. You haven't. He said you're the single only person who hasn't given up on him. That's all he needs to walk away from all of this. And now he finally has an opportunity to do that."

I wasn't sure exactly what Grady meant by that, that now Cole had an opportunity to get out. He already tried once, but was still sucked back in. I was fairly certain that Cole needed an entirely new life to get away from his past.

"I'm sorry about your window," he stated, redirecting the conversation. "I did have to bust the lock to get in, but I made a temporary fix. I'll show you before I go."

"And where exactly are you going?" I asked curiously. I wondered if he would be going back to wherever Cole was.

"To right one last wrong," he said surreptitiously. "I won't see Cole again, if that's what you're wondering. He's gone. He had to leave. I'm sure you'll get more information tomorrow when you go to Antonio's."

"What do you mean he's gone? What does that mean?" I asked, trying not to sound somewhat hysterical.

"I don't know where he's going, he wouldn't tell me much. But I imagine you'll find that out tomorrow. All will be fine, just have some faith," he answered with a smile. *Not a very credible thing out of a violent criminal's mouth.* "I'm glad I met you, Sydney," he said politely, standing up from my couch. His eyes softened as he spoke. "I'm sorry for so much. For all his flaws – I know those are because of me. I am so grateful he's found someone to love him in spite of all that. If there's a boy who ever deserved your goodness, he's the one."

He smiled at me and I blankly stared back at him. I had so many more questions for him, but I could tell he was done talking. He led me over to the window, showing me how to wedge a fork in the broken lock to keep it tight until I could get it fixed.

"I'll go out the back if you don't mind," he said softly. I nodded and he let himself out. I imagined that was the last time I would ever see Cole's father. It felt bittersweet in a way, to meet someone that played such a powerful role in Cole's life, even though it was such a sad story. But to see the emotion in his face when he talked about his past – I believed he did have some true regrets. No matter how bad of a man he was, I still harbored some hope deep down that perhaps someday they would have a chance to truly communicate their feelings to each other, however broken the conversation may be. There was so much healing that needed to be done, for both of them. I wondered if they would ever get to that point.

I checked all the locks in my house before heading upstairs to bed, just to make sure there would be no more surprises tonight. I took a long warm shower and the emotion and exhaustion I was holding onto ran over me along with the stream of water. I missed Sam tremendously. I missed my mom and felt heartbroken that of all times in my life I couldn't talk to her, I hated this is what she was missing. I needed her comfort so much. I even missed Ian in some ways - the simplicity of the way he loved me. It was never scary or complicated. It didn't challenge me either, but in so many ways it was just *easy*. I was so overwhelmed by everything that I longed for 'easy' in this moment. But I knew with Cole that wasn't even an option for me.

Cole. I couldn't get him off my mind as I lay awake in bed. I hated not knowing if he was okay. I hated the thought that he left town without me – that's what his father had suggested. Maybe after a lifetime of people giving up on him, maybe it was finally his turn – maybe he had given up on me.

I knew sleep wouldn't come. The nighttime noises outside my bedroom didn't provide any comfort. The silence in my room felt loud and chaotic and I needed a distraction. Despite the feeling in my stomach that it wasn't a good idea, I flipped on the TV.

"In breaking news tonight, a search is underway for several murder suspects related to an incident that occurred near Townsend Road in West Cove tonight," the brunette female reporter said into the camera. The graphics flashed to a dark warehouse-type building with yellow police tape all around. *"Several suspects are being pursued for the murder of Burton McClellan, and you are asked to call West Cove PD with any information you may have on the whereabouts of these four men..."* Four mug shots appeared on the screen one by one – the first two they flashed were unrecognizable, and I felt so relieved. The third picture they posted however, it sent chills through my entire body – it was a picture of Cole's father. I felt an immediate sense of fear all over again, knowing he was just in my apartment, alone with me, acting seemingly fine even though he may have just committed a major crime.

The last mug shot they posted though – I froze stiff.

Cole. It was Cole's face on my television, with a yellow scrolling banner underneath his photo. *Wanted for murder.*

I threw up in my bed.

CHAPTER 20

I didn't think sleep would find me, but apparently I cried so hard that my eyes gave up and I finally passed out. I awoke at seven a.m. to a buzzing cell phone, hoping so badly that the night before was all just a dream. But the pile of dirty sheets next to me on the floor and the way my eyes felt as though I'd been punched in the face – that all enforced my reality.

The text on the screen was from Dr. Nikki. *Saw the news this morning before work. Not sure what's going on, but please take whatever time you need. Call me if I can do anything to help.*

I immediately turned on the news, hoping for some update, particularly some confirmation they caught the real person responsible for the crime. Instead, the status was the same as the night before – all four men they showed previously were still suspects, and none of them had been found. My stomach was in knots and I wasn't sure what to even do.

Antonio's. Cole told me he would communicate with me through him, and Grady confirmed that. I wasn't sure what time I could go. They probably didn't even open until lunch time. How would I make it until then?

I took another shower, careful to wash off any remnants of my weak stomach from the night before. My nerves were on fire and my hands wouldn't stop shaking as I washed my hair. I was a complete and total mess.

Finally ten a.m. rolled around and I couldn't wait any longer. Surely Antonio had to get to his restaurant ahead of time to prep for the day, right? I couldn't stand waiting around my condo for another minute. I made the short ten minute drive towards West Cove, absentmindedly rubbing the silver ring attached to the necklace Cole gave me. *Just you and me.* Those word echoed in my brain. They were such short, simple words, but our situation did not mirror their simplicity.

I pulled into the parking lot of Antonio's restaurant, thankful to see one car already parked there around the back of the building. I parked mine in the front and walked up to the front door. It was still locked, but I gently knocked. Within seconds, I could see Antonio's face in the glass.

"Sydney," he said warmly as he unlocked the door and let me in. "How did you know to come here?" He locked the door behind us, checking first to make sure no one had followed me into the parking lot.

"A visitor came to my house last night," I said cautiously, not sure how much information to give. If Cole was really a wanted criminal, I didn't want to take my chances of giving out too much information. I wanted no part of it. "A man I'd never seen before." *That part was true.* "He told me to come here for information on Cole."

"Well I don't know how much information I have for you per se," he said, sounding somewhat disappointed. "I don't really know what happened, truth be told. I was just instructed to give you this." He reached behind the restaurant counter and pulled out a small, metal box. I recognized it from the first night Cole took me to his house – when we laid in the back of his truck, eating tacos. It had to be the same box. "He indicated you would know what to do with this?" He held the box out to me.

"There's a lock on it," I replied, taking the box from him. The lock had a three-digit number. They were currently all set to *000*. "Am I supposed to open this? What's the number?"

"All I was told is that you would know what to do," he shrugged. "You don't know the number?"

I tried thinking about it, but I didn't recall the box even having a lock on it when he showed it to me. How was I supposed to know the number?

"Is he okay? What did he say?" I pried, eager for some kind of good news.

"I don't know the situation," Antonio answered honestly. "Someone else dropped it off with that message." I wanted to ask him if that person was Cole's father, but I didn't want to bring him into the conversation. "Look, I don't want to rush you, but I think it's best if you leave. There may be people coming around, asking some questions. I don't think it would be wise for you to hang around here. Leave your number and I can contact you if I get any more information or correspondence from him, but I think that box is it."

I wrote my cell number down on a restaurant napkin, feeling disappointed by this entire exchange. I wanted so much more. I wanted to know Cole was okay, and more importantly where he was. I wanted to know if he had anything to do with what he was being accused of. Honestly I secretly hoped he would *be* there, hiding in the back, waiting to reassure me that everything would be okay.

"Thank you," I said sincerely, reaching out to give Antonio a hug.

"I think you're the only thing that boy loved more than my tacos," he teased, hugging me back. "If there's anything I can do, let me know. Think hard about the number on the lock. If he thinks you know it, then it must be in that pretty little head somewhere."

I flashed him a genuine smile and he led me out of the restaurant. I climbed back in my SUV trying to figure out a place to go. I ended up heading towards one of the smaller, less crowded beaches Sam and I used to frequent during the week. This early in the day I hoped I would have some solitude there.

Sure enough, I pulled onto the side of the road where people parked for Hidden Beach.

There was only one other car there, so I was thankful I would have some privacy. I made the short walk down the dirt path, carrying the metal box. I finally made it to the beach and opted to climb up some of the big boulders in the sand. The sun felt warm on my skin and I was thankful for the openness of this spot. I didn't feel as cramped and afraid and alone as I did in my condo, yet I had the privacy I needed for this moment.

I sat on top of one of the giant boulders with the metal box in my lap. What three numbers would Cole pick for his lock? More importantly, how would he expect me to know the number? I tried to recall the tattoos on his chest. I had seen them so many times, but I can't say I memorized all of them. Usually my mind was elsewhere when he had his shirt off. One of the numbers I remembered was the date Harvey became his guardian… What was that, *413*? I entered in those numbers, but the lock didn't open. There was also the date of his motorcycle accident, but I couldn't quite envision it. It started with an *8*… I couldn't recall the rest. What other date would've been important? Better yet, which one would he think I'm sure about? I rubbed the ring around my neck between my fingers, and finally it came to me.

The day we met. Cole was sentimental about time, obviously, the way he marked his body with important dates the way he did. *July 7th,* could that be it? I moved the numbers on the lock until it read *707*. The lock immediately popped open.

I sucked in a breath, surprised that worked, but nervous to see what was inside. There was still a sizeable roll of money – I wasn't sure how much it was, and I was too uncomfortable to count it here, but it looked like a lot. I was unsure why he wouldn't have taken that with him, but then again, I wasn't sure what had happened. I rummaged through the rest of the box. The brochures about the land and the realtor's business card, those were still in there – but there was one thing I hadn't noticed when he first showed me the box.

I pulled out a ticket of some sort – *San Diego Padres* – was this a ticket for a baseball game? One ticket? I smiled as I held it in my hands. Maybe he really did like baseball more than I thought when we first met. I couldn't stop beaming, thinking back to that first night at my house when he told me we'd already made it to third base. I loved his sense of humor immediately. That was one of the first things that drew me to him.

I studied the ticket. *September 9th, 7:00pm.* Wait a minute, that hadn't happened yet – it was only September 3rd today. I flipped the ticket over, noticing his handwriting on the back. *You and me - and baseball.* My mouth curled up into a smile. I rummaged through the rest of the box, and at the bottom, there was an envelope with my name on it. I quickly broke the seal and pulled out a folded piece of paper.

Sydney – I know I'm probably not the guy you always imagined you would love. I'm not the prince your mom probably read you fairytales about when you were little, and I know I'm definitely not the kind of guy any father would choose for you. I have scars. I have flaws. I have an imperfect past that I completely regret. I know I may not be what you imagined for the rest of your life – but you are in every way the only girl I've ever really fallen for. Only you could love an imperfect man so perfectly. I've never seen goodness in anyone like I see it in you. It's like your heart is on the outside where everyone can see it, whereas I've spent a lifetime hiding mine. But you've changed all that for me – I have nothing to hide from you.

I imagine you're hearing some unfavorable things about me now – but with you, I have no secrets. Maybe I've done what they say I've done, or maybe I haven't – but either way you'll have to decide what you do or don't want to know – and whether that changes whether or not I'm worthy of the way you feel about me.

All I know is from the moment I saw you until the last moment you walked away from me, I want no part of this world without you. So you have a choice to make. Maybe it's selfish of me to ask this of you, I don't know, but the choice is yours, Syd. If you want to live your life with me –

if you want to spend our days laughing together in the sand, and our nights loving each other under the perfect night sky – then come and get me. There's a ticket in here and everything you need. But if you have any regrets over loving me as I am, even a single hesitation – I'll understand when I see the empty seat beside me and I'll forever wish for you to have the exact kind of life you truly want and deserve. The money in the box – I don't need it. It's yours. You can use it to start your animal sanctuary, or use it for the therapy you'll need after all I've put you through. Just know that I am grateful for every moment we had together, whether I get more, or if this is it. But I will forever be thankful for the day you rescued me – 707.

Love,

Cole

I wiped all of the wet tears off my face, smiling and sobbing all at the same time. He somehow made me feel every emotion possible. There was a one way plane ticket enclosed with the envelope, and I had so much in my head. He was right – maybe he did something horrible, and maybe he didn't. But ultimately did I want to know? Would it change my feelings about him?

I strangely thought about Ian in that moment. When he talked about spending our life together, I hesitated – I panicked, unsure his life was right for me. It was big and meticulously planned, which should have sounded wonderful, but it was the life *he* wanted and I felt lost in that. I hesitated because I feared I was giving up myself just to be with him. With Cole though, it felt so different. I didn't feel like I could even choose a life with him or without him – without him wasn't an option in my brain.

Sam pointed out once that the only two men who ever really loved me, they did it in such different ways – Ian was safe and cautious and he adored me. I knew that was true. But Cole, he loved me with such an unrelenting fierceness – like nothing circumstantial could ever change the way he felt about me – as if his feelings were an absolute truth that could never be rescinded or changed. That kind of love knew no hesitation. There was no turning back from it, or getting over it. Once it hit you, it set you on fire and that's the only way you could ever be loved again. I knew with absolute certainty that no other man could ever love me the way he did.

I knew exactly what I had to do in that moment. I pulled out my cell phone and called the airline's number listed on the plane ticket – and cancelled the reservation.

CHAPTER 21

Instead of driving back to my condo, I drove straight to the vet clinic. I knew I needed to talk to Dr. Nikki right away. My face was probably a swollen, puffy mess from all my tears over the last twelve hours, but I didn't care.

As soon as I walked in the clinic, Eva shot me a sympathetic glance. For once in all the time I knew her, she said nothing. I headed straight to the back, thankful to see Dr. Nikki washing up after having completed a surgery.

"Give me just a minute," she said warmly as soon as I walked by the operating room. I headed towards her office, sitting back down in one of those yellow chairs I occupied just yesterday afternoon.

My head still felt a little cloudy with everything going on, but I felt like I at least had more clarity now than I had just an hour earlier. Finally Dr. Nikki made her way into the room, but instead of sitting behind her desk, she sat down in the chair right next to me and put a soft hand on my knee.

"How are you holding up?" she asked sincerely.

"I'm fine," I shrugged, not wanting to really get into too many details. "I think I'm going to need some time off," I said hesitantly.

"Of course, whatever you need," she said softly.

"Honestly I'm not sure when I'll be back," I explained vaguely. "I, um, may need you to take the two cats I still have…" I wasn't sure what else to tell her.

"Say no more, take as much time as you need," she repeated, picking up on my hesitation. "I'll send Eva to get the cats this afternoon. Do whatever you need to do."

I squeezed her hand, thankful to have her support without having to answer any questions.

"I just have one thing I was wondering about," I stated before getting up to leave. "When you found that litter of puppies on the side of the road, did you know immediately what to do?"

"Of course not," she replied with a smile. "I had no clue. But I saw something worth rescuing and I knew I had no other choice. Sometimes you're not the one choosing. Sometimes you're the one being *chosen.*"

"Thank you," I said genuinely, standing up from the chair. She embraced me in a huge, warm hug, and I wondered if she sensed the possibility that we wouldn't see each other again for quite a long time.

"Call me when things settle," she said, escorting me out. I waved goodbye and left the clinic, a slow tear rolling down my cheek at the thought of that being my final exit.

I drove back home and grabbed a large suitcase. I looked around my condo, taking inventory of what was essential and what wasn't. My place came furnished when I signed the rental agreement, so most of the big stuff wasn't mine anyway. I loaded up the suitcase with some of my favorite clothes, my toiletries, an old photograph book, and a few other personal items. Everything else at the moment looked unimportant.

I loaded up my vehicle, filled it up with gas at the nearest station, and then hit the highway. I flipped open Cole's metal box, pulling out the brochures of land in southern California. I found an address and typed it into my GPS.

That was it. I was headed south.

About seven long, slow hours into my drive, I couldn't take it anymore. I was exhausted and the sun had set, and I was afraid I would fall asleep at the wheel. That wouldn't have done me any favors. I eventually pulled over into the lot of a small but well lit hotel and got a room for the night.

I wasn't sure I'd ever stayed in a hotel room by myself before. It felt a little creepy, but I was so tired, it didn't bother me as much as it probably would've otherwise. I took a long, hot shower, checking my phone repeatedly on the chance anyone tried to call. The screen remained blank and my disappointment returned. Maybe I was crazy for doing this. Maybe I should've waited the six days until I could've used the plane ticket. But then I realized that wasn't the point. I couldn't possibly wait six more days, it would've been pure torture. Maybe I didn't exactly have a plan, but doing *something* felt better than just *waiting.*

I slept for a glorious nine hours, waking up feeling refreshed and ready to complete my drive. I called the number for the realtor on the business card in Cole's box. I wondered what I even planned to say to him, but I was prepared to just kind of wing it.

"Sanderson Realty, this is Mike," a voice said on the other end.

"Hi, uh, hello, my name is Sydney and I am calling on a property you have listed," I explained, trying to sound put together and somewhat professional. I read him the address off of one of the brochures.

"Ah, sorry, that one has already been picked up," Mike said, sounding disappointed. "That deal was in the works for awhile, but it's done. That property's gone. Must be an old brochure you have, I apologize for that," he said courteously. "I do have some others in the same price range though."

"I'm not sure I'm interested in another property, that's the only one I'm familiar with," I stated, unsure of where to even go from here. "Are there others around that one for sale?"

"None like that property, it was almost ten acres," he said with a low whistle. "You can't find that kind of real estate around here. That was a once in a lifetime kind of purchase. The guy who bought it wanted some ponies for his daughter or something, there's nowhere else like that even close. But I do have some one to two acre parcels if you're just looking at building a house?"

"I think I'm fine for now, but thank you for your time," I said politely, hanging up the phone. *Ponies.* All of that wasted space so some rich girl could have a few horses to forget about as she grew up. I slammed my fist on the steering wheel, completely annoyed that nothing was going my way. I cranked up the stereo, drowning my frustrations in loud music.

I headed towards the address in my GPS anyway, unsure of where else to go. I figured I would just get a hotel around there and a good night's sleep, and maybe my head would feel better in the morning. Only five more days left until the baseball game, that was a plus. But those were going to be long, awkward days to fill. I wasn't even sure what I was doing here anymore.

Eventually I pulled off the highway and down a long, dirt road. I smirked as I could see the ocean in the distance, just like Cole talked about. It was a beautiful spot. There were fruit trees everywhere, and the land looked so spacious, yet simple. It looked majestic on its own, but also looked like it was yearning for life – for footprints in the dirt and hands working in the soil. Towards the far end of the property, it looked like there was already a camper of sorts set up. *Probably a camper filled with ponies,* I snickered. As I got closer, I felt like a trespasser, but I really wasn't sure where else to go. I noticed a motorcycle propped up next to the camper.

My heart began thumping loudly in my chest.

An outside light came on and I saw the front door of the camper open up. A large, shirtless man stepped out the front door, pulling on a tight v-neck t-shirt as I pulled up closer. I could see tattoos across his chest and down his biceps, and I swear my heart skipped a beat. He stepped down the camper steps and into the dirt area where I pulled my SUV up.

It was in that moment I realized this guy had darker hair than Cole. He also appeared to be a little bit shorter, although he was still a huge guy. I also noticed the motorcycle against the camper was a deep blue – not grey like Cole's bike. Disappointment washed over me and I wanted to cry.

The guy walked over to my driver's side door and I debated throwing the car in reverse. Being alone in the middle of nowhere with a large unrecognizable man didn't seem like the best choice. But something about the way he looked at me as he approached, that was enough to make me stay put and roll down the window.

"Holy shit, what are you doing here?" the guy said in disbelief.

"I'm sorry, I think I took a wrong turn," I lied, unsure as to why he was looking at me the way he was.

"You don't remember me from the bonfire a couple months back? I'm Bryce," he smirked.

"Wait, you know Cole?" I said in complete shock. His face maybe looked a little familiar as I stared at him, but I had met so many people that night.

"Isn't that why you're here?" he said, raising up his arms, gesturing towards the camper and the land all around him. I nodded slowly, completely confused by what was happening. "Why are you here already? He told me you weren't coming until next Wednesday. I don't have everything ready yet."

"I don't understand, this property is sold already," I began, turning off my car engine. "Are you sure you're supposed to be here?"

"I'm sanding down a sign with your name on it as we speak, I promise I'm a welcome guest," he shrugged with a smile, motioning for me to step out of the car.

I climbed out of my SUV, still unsure of what was happening. "Is Cole here?" I asked nervously. I had a feeling if he was, he would've already come out of the camper.

"No," he replied calmly, shaking his head. "I haven't heard from him yet." He furrowed his brow and I wonder what all he knew. "How did you know to come here? Cole told me about his plans, but he said you'd be meeting him at a baseball game next week. I'm just here setting everything up."

"I was too impatient to wait until next week," I shrugged. "Cole always talked about this land, so I headed south. But this morning I called the realtor and he told me this property already sold to some guy with ponies."

"Harvey," he mumbled with a slight laugh. "His gambling… Every time he won big, people would ask him what he was going to do with the money. He always said he wanted to buy some ponies – race horses."

"So Harvey bought this land?" I asked, still trying to sort everything out.

"I don't know the details, but I imagine he had a hand in it," Bryce explained. "Harvey isn't the greatest guy, you probably know that by now. But he loves big. Especially when it comes to Cole. I wouldn't be surprised at all if he had something to do with all this."

Honestly I wasn't sure what to think – I still had no idea what kind of man Harvey was. I knew how he felt for Cole, that was unmistakable, but to say whether or not he was a good man, that seemed indecipherable. Grady suggested Harvey was the deceitful one, but I knew I couldn't trust either of them on that.

"Do you know what happened last night?" I asked bluntly. I so badly wanted information.

"I know some of it," he said honestly, "and I have some assumptions on the rest. I've been around West Cove for a long time. It seems like there are a lot of secrets, but in the light of day, it's not so secret. Everyone does what they have to in order to keep their heads up. They're all hungry for power, and I don't blame them, it's hard not to get sucked into that when life around you is otherwise shit. Kids growing up around there, they know they're different. They know they don't have the same options as the Ridge City kids, so they emulate their parents. They see ways to make money, despite what comes with that, and they get recruited. Cole never stood a chance, and he knew that from a young age."

"What about you?" I asked softly as we walked towards the camper. "Are you involved in all that? You work at the bike shop, don't you?"

"Yeah, part-time," he explained. "I'm actually taking a couple classes at the community college in town, but no one knows that. I'm just at the bike shop to keep up appearances. But I'm fortunate, I don't have to work as hard as all the other young guys in West Cove. I have immunity."

"How on earth do you earn that?" I questioned, unsure if he would even tell me.

"Easy, I knew one of the biggest secrets in West Cove until it all came out last night," he shrugged. "You probably know by now that Harvey had a son before Cole, right?"

I nodded, surprised he was being this forthcoming with me.

"Well, I know who killed him. It was reported as a drunk driver, a hit and run. But I am one of the only people who knows the truth. I know who did it."

"Grady," I said quietly, assuming I also knew the secret after Harvey finally let it out the other night.

"Cole's biological dad?" Bryce scoffed. "He had nothing to do with it. That's the kicker. Everyone is always pointing their fingers at the wrong people to use it to their advantage. Cole's father wasn't a good man by any stretch, but he's not the villain Harvey sold to you."

"Then who did it?" I questioned, unsure he would even tell me.

"The one person you wouldn't suspect. It was Harvey himself."

CHAPTER 22

My head was spinning and I felt like I would never truly understand the tangled web of West Cove. None of it made any sense.

"Why would Harvey commit a crime like that, and blame someone else?" I said naïvely. Maybe that was a dumb thing to ask, but it just didn't make sense.

"Because guilt like that isn't easily overcome," Bryce replied, leading me into the camper. Sadly I understood exactly what he meant. Guilt like that could certainly turn even the best person into someone else. "Harvey wasn't a good man before, according to my father," he continued. "But after that incident – it completely changed him. As far as I know, even his wife has no idea. It was truly just an accident, but obviously it weighed so heavily on him. He was out for blood, as if the world owed him something. When Cole entered their lives, he became even more intense. Like a man willingly giving up his own child should be punished far worse than one who lost his child by his own hands, however accidental it was. He wanted Grady to pay for that, for abandoning Cole the way he did, but he already had his own troubles and got picked up for arson before Harvey could even do anything about him."

It all started making a little more sense to me as he spoke. I didn't know how Harvey lived with such a secret though. I couldn't imagine spending a lifetime knowing you'd done something like that. My situation with Ian, I felt the guilt for it, sure. And it ate at me every single day. But having people around me telling me it wasn't my fault, even though I didn't believe them, it was still probably the only thing that kept me remotely sane during that period in my life.

"Why are you telling me all this?" I asked curiously, surprised I was finding out more from this stranger than what I'd learned from Cole or even Harvey himself. Although apparently Cole didn't seem to even know the big picture before whatever went down.

"Because there needs to be an end to it," he sighed. "And Cole is doing it. He's finally getting out from all of it. All because of a girl," he smiled.

"I don't think it's because of me," I blushed. "He wanted all this before he met me."

"Wanting something and actually going after it are two very different things," he replied. "Everyone in West Cove wants something. More money, more notoriety, a completely different life… Don't underestimate your role in this. Offering someone goodness the way you do, that changes people more than the secrets around us ever could. He told me what you did for Crazy Jamie," he said, clearing his throat. The mention of her caught me off guard. Why would Cole mention something like that to him? I stared blankly at him.

"There was one West Cove secret I didn't know until last night. I'm not sure anyone knew. But it turns out Crazy Jamie – that's his biological mom."

I gasped, probably audibly, completely in shock. That didn't seem possible.

"She didn't even recognize him when he approached her that night, and he had no idea himself. You, she remembered, but the son she gave up on – she had no idea. But you forced him into sharing your faith in people and I think it really caught him off guard. He said goodness like that, from a girl like you, offering it to someone who doesn't deserve it, that's the only thing that can save this world. That's why he won't let you go," he shrugged. "That's why he did whatever it took to get out of the life he was in."

"Do you think he really did what the news said he did?" I asked quietly. I figured while he was laying it all out, I may as well ask, though I wasn't sure how ready I was to hear that answer.

"Does it matter to you?" he asked directly. I thought about it as he spoke. "Don't make his guilt your own, no matter what he's done."

I understood what he was saying, but it was still so big to me. It felt like a cloud that would always be hanging over us.

"Use everything he's done wrong, all of the money, the resources you've been given… Use it for good," he stated. "I'm not saying that can undo anything that's been done. It doesn't right those wrongs, or fix anything, but it's the only way to move on."

His words resonated with me. I believed that. No matter what Cole had been through, I certainly didn't believe it was too late for him. And by now there was no use blaming anyone else for it all – the shortcomings of his parents, the circumstances he was forced into, the guilt Harvey hung on to just to pour into someone else to make up for his inability to forgive himself – it was finally time to move on from all of that.

I offered a weary smile to Bryce, exhausted from this day and this intense conversation. "I should probably go find a hotel," I stated, noticing it was already almost nine p.m.

"You're welcome to stay here," he offered, motioning around the camper. It was definitely dated and worn, but it was very clean and organized. It was much larger inside than what I first pictured when I drove up. "There's a bedroom in the back you can have to yourself. I just need to move something. This table here folds out into a bed, so I'll sleep there if that doesn't make you too uncomfortable."

It did seem like an odd arrangement, but it also seemed like a lot less trouble than having to find a hotel room this late. Bryce seemed genuine and kind, and he was obviously doing something nice for Cole by being here. "That sounds great actually," I stated with relief in my voice. "I'll go grab my bag."

I headed out to my car, grabbing just the essentials, and headed back in the camper. Bryce was holding a large wooden board of some sort, but I could only see the back of it.

"I'm not sure I'm supposed to show you this yet, it was supposed to be a surprise," he blushed. "Cole's orders."

"Then it can wait," I said with a smile, wondering what they were up to. "When do you think he'll come? I don't want to bother you here while I wait for him, I can head back into town tomorrow to find a place until he arrives."

"I'm actually planning on heading out tomorrow myself," he shrugged. "My work here is almost done. You can stay. Just no peeking. I think he wanted a more dramatic surprise for you. Yet ironically I think you may be the one surprising him."

"I just hope he comes," I said quietly, still a bit nervous about the entire thing. I couldn't imagine what he was dealing with right now, with his face all over the news. I wondered where he went last night.

"He'll come," Bryce said reassuringly. "That's the one thing about Cole. Sometimes he's an asshole, and he's got a hell of a right hook, but he always lives up to his word. He'll come."

I said goodnight, making my way into the back bedroom of the camper. I changed into some sleep clothes, thankful I brought some actual yoga pants to wear instead of the short shorts Cole saw me in the first night we'd met. I laid down, replaying so much of the time we'd spent together in my mind, longing for the chance to continue all of that. Within a few minutes, I drifted off into a deep, restful sleep.

A loud buzzing sound woke up me. The clock next to the bed read five-thirty. I quickly grabbed my phone off the side table, assuming that's where the sound was coming from. It took me a minute to realize the noise was actually coming from outside the camper.

A motorcycle.

I stood up immediately, quickly trying to throw on the wedge sandals I had on the night before. I ran out the camper door in my yoga pants, a camisole, and my wedge heels, probably looking completely ridiculous. A grey motorcycle pulled up to the trailer.

My heart sped up and I felt delirious. The sun wasn't even up yet, but between the moon and the small outside light attached to the camper, it was enough. I could see Cole perfectly as he shut off the engine of his bike.

"Sydney?" he said in shock, probably quite surprised to see me. He climbed off his bike, walking towards me. "What are you doing here?"

"You asked me in your letter to come and get you," I said with a playful shrug. "I wasn't sure where else to find you, other than under some avocado trees."

He walked up to me and put a firm arm around my waist, pulling me in and kissing me with even more intensity than I expected.

"I thought we were still working our way around the bases," he teased as he slowly pulled his face away from mine. "I thought we were meeting by home plate. I didn't think I would see you before then."

"You're home base for me," I whispered. He kissed me again and I knew everything was falling into place. This moment, standing in the dirt with his arms wrapped around me, it felt more like home than anything I'd felt before.

"The sign, Bryce," Cole said loudly, banging on the camper door. He must've known he was still there from his motorcycle parked out front by Cole's.

Bryce came scurrying out, holding the large wooden board he had last night. He looked ridiculous in his sweat pants, no shirt, and grey slippers as he quickly attached the board to a small pole that had been placed outside the camper.

"There's just one thing," Cole said mischievously. "I made a promise to you. Just you and me, remember?"

"Are you saying you want Bryce to live with us too in this beautiful camper?" I teased.

"I'm just saying I don't want you to be alone with me," he replied with a smirk. He led me over to the wooden sign where Bryce stood beaming, admiring his work.

Sydney's Animal Sanctuary. It was carved into the wood and it was absolutely beautiful.

A slow tear crept out of the corner of my eye. "Really?" I said in disbelief.

"We can change the name if you want," he shrugged. "But it's a start. I already have all the permits, I've been working on those for awhile. So maybe it's not just you and me, but also every creature you come across that you just can't say no to."

"Why are you doing all of this for me?"

"Because you rescued me," he said quietly. "And I know you're not done yet."

I stared into his eyes as the sun started slowly creeping up over the horizon. There were so many unspoken words between us here in this moment – I had so many questions, and wanted to know so much about where he'd been and about what truly happened. But I knew that no matter what he'd done, that's not who he was to me. He was simply just the guy I'd fallen for, and he was standing here in front of me giving me everything I'd ever wanted. I fell for him as innocently as any girl should fall for a boy – he made me laugh, promised to keep me safe from the cruelty of the world, and he loved me as fiercely as any man could. That was everything a girl needed. For the first time in my life, *I* felt rescued. And I knew no matter what his past looked like, this was our beginning.

EPILOGUE

"Are you ready to come in for dinner yet?" I asked as Cole was still out hammering away on the roof of our soon-to-be ready house. He spent long hours working on it when he wasn't down at the bike shop. We were still living in the camper while he finished up the house.

"It depends, are we having tacos?" he smirked.

"No, pasta," I replied, smiling at the fact that Cole really did buy me a pasta maker. He gave it to me as a wedding present after we left the courthouse, right before we headed to my first *San Diego Padres* game. I mentioned the pasta maker once in passing, and he never forgot. He was amazing like that. The 300 pairs of shoes I also mentioned, however, he wanted to debate, but I was okay with his hesitation on that.

"Did you already do the evening feeding?" he asked, climbing down the ladder. Cole built a small barn and put up a bunch of fences for me before he even started working on our house.

"Of course, the pigs all got their pellets, the two horses got their hay, the goats got last night's leftovers and the cats are ignoring me, so they can catch the barn mice until they want to apologize," I shrugged.

Sure enough, Cole worked tirelessly to give me everything I dreamed of. He bought a great building space in town to start up his own motorcycle repair shop, and he was already bringing in good business with that. He worked on our house in his spare time, set back on our property with a perfect view of the ocean in the distance just like we'd talked about all those months ago.

The animal sanctuary took off quickly, and I had Dr. Nikki to thank for that. As soon as I told her I wouldn't make it back to the clinic, she didn't hesitate to offer me all the help she could with the rescue. She had even been out to visit a couple times to help me with some of the logistics and I was so grateful for her help.

The situation back home in Mountain Ridge had largely resolved shortly after it all went down, but we both had no desire to go back. This was our life now, and we were so happy. Cole's father, Grady, ended up taking the fall for the entire thing. I wasn't convinced he was solely responsible for it all, but Cole and I never brought it up. It really didn't matter, but the conversation I had with Cole's father that night after it all went down, it replayed in my mind often. He said he had one last right to wrong, and I always wondered if that meant setting Cole free from the consequences of Grady abandoning him in the first place. I wondered if that was his last attempt at Cole's forgiveness – taking the fall for him just to release him from all the wrongdoings he suffered as a result of the hands Grady left him in.

Cole came in for dinner and as he sat down at the table, I quietly faced him with a serious expression. "I have to tell you something," I said, my voice full of emotion.

"What is it?" he asked with concern.

I unhooked the silver necklace from around my neck, the one he gave me back when we were still dating. I slid the ring off the chain, slowly pushing it towards him across the table. "I can't do this anymore. You and me… It's over." A slow tear slid down my cheek and Cole looked panicked.

"What's wrong? What happened?" he said, reaching out for my hand. "Whatever it is, we can get through it. Together."

"Good, because this baby needs a father," I said, finally turning my lips up into a smile. I pulled an ultrasound picture out of my lap and slid it across the table towards him. "There's no more you and me." I paused for dramatic effect. "There's going to be one more."

Cole's face immediately lit up, and he stood up from the table, pulling me into his arms.

"Seriously?" he exclaimed, still beaming as he held me tight. "Oh, Syd. Really?"

"Yes," I replied, kissing him tenderly. "But we still have a few months before finding out if it's a boy or girl."

"I don't care what it is, there's only one thing that matters," he said softly.

"That the baby is healthy, I know," I snickered.

"That's not what I was going to say at all," he replied, his lips curling up into a grin. He gently lifted my face up towards him. "This baby has to love tacos and baseball."

I smiled, tracing my finger around the latest tattoo on Cole's arm. It was a baseball diamond with the date *707* on it.

"I think no matter what, the baby will look up to his father," I said sincerely.

Cole scooped me up and carried me to the back of the camper, trailing kisses down my neck.

I never had those dreams of falling ever again – those ones that enveloped me in fear of failure and uncertainty after Ian. I suppose that was because I wasn't falling at all anymore – I had been caught by these arms that promised me I'd be the girl he'd love forever. No more hesitation – just pigs, a pasta maker, and a man to love me the rest of my life. The only thing I had left to want were the shoes… But I didn't care how long I had to wait for that. I learned love wasn't about choosing someone perfect – but rather about loving someone's imperfections perfectly, despite their circumstances – and Cole was every bit of imperfection worth falling for. Not someone to give up on, or change my mind on – no, he was the best kind of man to love – *the falling kind.*

About the Author

Randileigh Kennedy grew up in Nevada and now resides in the Midwest. When she isn't writing, she stays busy planning random theme parties and working on crafty DIY projects, which are all featured on her blog: www.randileighkennedy.com.

You can also follow her on social media (Facebook – Randileigh Kennedy, and Twitter - @randileighk) - but expect more pictures of her mini pig Kevin Bacon than you'll see of her human children and insanely handsome husband.

If you enjoyed this book, please make sure you leave a review on Amazon.com – your feedback helps out tremendously.

Be sure to check out other books from Randileigh, including *Ten Seconds of Crazy*, along with the *Six Series*, all available at Amazon.com. For more information, you can visit her Amazon author page at http://www.amazon.com/-/e/BooJHoFMQQ.